Winter King

by

Anne Stevens

Murder in Henry's Court
(Tudor Crimes Book I)

Foreword

It is the Year of Our Lord 1529....

All nations, should they wish to be considered as great, must be governed by leaders of true ability. Often, these great men came from humble beginnings, and rose to pre-eminence using not only their intelligence, but their native wit and cunning.

Amongst the great men of England none have risen higher from the ranks, or become a greater statesman, than Cardinal Thomas Wolsey. His climb to becoming King Henry VIII's foremost minister of state is steady, yet seemingly unstoppable. The Cardinal has guided his king from youth, to adulthood, through the bright, early years of promise, and scholarly achievement. He is always there, beside Christendom's most beloved ruler.

The years pass, and Henry's private life turns him from 'Bluff King Hal' into a man of moods, and sudden angers. He is set on having a son, for his own sake, and for that of the realm. Queen Katherine is grown old, and it is unlikely she will ever provide a legitimate heir to the English throne.

Henry must have his way, of course, yet Thomas Wolsey seems unable to oblige him by arranging a simple annulment. In Rome, Pope Clement, a corrupt old man, baulks the cardinal at every turn, until, at last, Henry has had enough. After listening to his closest advisor, the Duke of Norfolk, and his mistress, Anne Boleyn, the king agrees that Wolsey is to be stripped of all of his titles, and finally, in the year 1530, his enemies will feel strong enough to strike at him with impunity. The great man's fall from grace will be spectacular.

Lesser men must fill the gap left by the cardinal, and a struggle for power is inevitable. It is a time when men of low birth can try their luck, and match themselves against the highest in the land, in a quest for their place in history. Some men will only serve, and others, like Thomas Cromwell, the Percy family, Norfolk, with his Howard clan, and the wastrel Duke of Suffolk, Charles Brandon, will use them ruthlessly.

Henry's ship of state is now rudderless, and will flounder without a strong hand at the tiller. The King might well rule by divine right, but he needs strong men, seasoned soldiers, men of law, and clever clerics to support him. Without such support, England might well degenerate into bloody civil war again.

Once, it was all done by one brilliant man ... Cardinal Thomas Wolsey, and the king will regret his passing with every ensuing moment, despite allowing it to come about. Even at the very end of his life, Wolsey cannot understand how he has failed his beloved master, and believes he will be forgiven.

Having carefully guided Henry through the Spring and Summer of his reign, the cleric fails to see that his unforgiving lord is changed for ever. He is now an altogether colder, more dangerous man, who vacillates between being his own man, and forgiving his old cardinal.

Whilst Tom Cromwell remains loyal to Wolsey, there are too many envious people willing to drag him down, so that they might steal his power. Little do they realise that the brooding king can hide behind several faces. To Norfolk and his kind, he remains open, and genial... but his other face is one of spite, and he has a self serving nature.

If Cardinal Wolsey is to be reprieved, Henry must have his pound of flesh. Wolsey is kept in a sort of limbo, never knowing how the king will think from day to day. Cromwell hears whispers of forgiveness from some quarters, and dire threats from others.

Ultimately, it is Henry who will decide, and the man who can whisper into his ear will have untold amounts of power. Whilst great men vie for their place at court, others come from lowlier backgrounds, and find themselves involved in a world of intrigue, casual death, and rapid advancement.

Few know what the future holds, but the man who rules the king can rule England. It just takes one clever individual to understand that Henry has become.... The Winter King.

1 The Bounty Man

The horse has been a fine acquisition for Captain Will Draper. Its broad, barrel chest and short, sturdy legs bar it from being fit for use in the lists, of course, but compensate for such a lordly shortcoming in every other way. The solidly framed Welsh Cob is, to the soldier's mind, well worth the small danger to his life she caused.

The Welsh, ever a troublesome race, had become loyal to the crown, since the Tudors came to the English throne, with the odd exception. Now and then, some lesser lord, grown discontent with his five hundred acres, sheep, and ill fortified stone house, would foment local troubles, hoping to benefit from an old feud or land dispute.

The first Tudor king, Henry VII, had been thrifty enough to stand down his vast paid armies, but shrewd enough to know that the odd rebellious Welshman would still have to be dealt with. To counter these sporadic threats, Henry adopted the policy of offering a bounty to those willing to do the crown's dirty work.

The King thus avoided paying for a standing army, and had no need to find gold, except upon the occasion of a satisfactory result. His son, the eighth Henry, recognises the worth of his father's actions, and so continues the custom during his own reign.

Men such as Will Draper are well enough suited by the casual arrangement, and will band together when necessary. Sometimes Will joins a bounty chase with a few others, and hunts down miscreants for an equal share of the spoils, and whatever goods they may plunder from the outlawed men. The tracking down of the better led bandit gangs often takes months, and usually ends in a bloody fight, often to the death.

The life of a bounty hunter can be well rewarded, but rather brief, often ending with one's own comrades dividing your meagre estate amongst the survivors of a skirmish. Will Draper knows all this, and understands the danger, but it is what he can do. He can fight, and he is wise enough to outthink the criminal mind. His time as a soldier in Ireland has served him well.

This latest foray sees Will Draper and seven other, similarly qualified, men set out to corner Lord Owen Gryffid. and bring his marauding war band to book. The malcontent Welshman, with a dozen followers, had burned farms, raped and robbed, across the bleak centre of the principality for six long months. Draper and his band almost give up hope of running him down ... but only almost.

The marauding Welshmen are trapped now, in a narrow snow filled valley and, with reluctance, they turn to fight the men who have dogged their trail for so long. Will dismounts from the sway backed, almost dead pony that has carried him across the mountains, and draws his sword. It is going to be a bloody morning's work, and he is eager to have it all done before the biting cold Welsh air which is frosting his breath, freezes his very lungs, and kills him.

The Welsh lord, Owen Gryffid is tired too. He has ridden far enough, and now he will stand and fight. There is no way out of the valley now, and there is no other option open to him. He will charge at the head of his men, and try to break through to open ground, where they can scatter to the four winds.

Will Draper sees his enemy make his dispositions, and knows there is a wild charge coming at any moment. If that happens, and the Welsh break through to the open ground behind, Will thinks, six months work will be for nought. The young man knows this, and so do the men who fan out on either side of him.

Win, or die is the order of the day. A simple enough thing for desperate men to understand, he thinks. It is no matter, either way. To let the Welshmen escape now, means slow starvation before Spring has a chance to arrive and warm their backs. Will raises his sword to his lips, and kisses the silver cross fastened to its hilt.

"God be with you, lads," Will mutters, and some of them cross themselves, despite never having been in a church since their baptism. There are no atheists when in the heat of battle, and these simple men hope that God is English on this particular day.

Men who have fought in the heat of battle will tell how the shouting will stop after the first, headlong, rush. They will shake their heads, knowingly, and explain that you need save all your breath just to stay alive. A seasoned fighter will always stand his ground, and set about his bloody business in near silence.

Though outnumbered, Will's party are stronger, better fed, and better armed. Two of his number have clumsy crossbows, and the Welsh hang back until they discharge their quarrels to no effect. The bolts fly harmlessly over the outlaws heads. The

Welsh chieftain does not flinch as one bolt
misses him by a hand's breadth, and he
raises his sword high, then shouts. The order,
in a guttural tongue, raises a frenzied cheer.

The Welsh surge forward, covering
the intervening ground in great bounds. Then
they are at each other in true earnest. Steel
bites into steel, and rips through flesh and
bone, filling the narrow valley with the
sound, and the sickly scent of death. It is a
brutal and bloody morning's work, as Will
Draper and his men fight for their prize; a
shared bounty of twenty English pounds.

The Welshmen know that there will
be no quarter given, and fight like demons
against the battle hardened English veterans.
To lay down your arms means either a
dagger thrust, and swift death, or surrender
and the gallows at the next court sessions in
Hereford. The two sides, armed with swords,
daggers and axes, lay into one another with a
terrible vigour that soon leaves many dead
and wounded, spilling their blood onto the
virgin white snow.

Will Draper knows his business well
and, armed with sword and knife, parries and
cuts with cold precision. Beside him, Tam
Shaw loses his footing on the treacherous
Welsh ice, and takes a savage sword slash

that bites deep into neck and sinew. Even as he dies, Will Draper thrusts his own blade into the killer's throat. The man staggers back, clawing at the jagged rip, trying to hold in his own precious blood. He spins around, spraying gore across all around him, and sinks to the snow, like a slowly wilting flower.

The young Englishman takes the force of an axe blow on his knife hilt, and quickly ripostes, plunging a foot of tempered steel into an unguarded chest. He twists the sword, so that it rips open the man's heart, pulls it free and turns to face the next attacker. The Welsh fight well, and have numbers on their side, but they are badly disciplined, and can not hold their ranks. Slowly, they are forced back to the head of the valley, stumbling over their own dead, where they finally break, and try to run for their lives.

Will Draper's fellow bounty hunters have lost two of their own number, and are not in any mood to show mercy as they press home the attack. One Welshman, a boy of, perhaps fifteen, drops his sword as a sign of surrender. He sees the look of anger on his enemy's face and manages to cross himself, just as he is hacked to the ground. The boy falls down onto one knee and throws up a hand to defend himself. The second blow hacks through his arm, and the third crushes his skull to a bloody pulp.

Owen Gryffid, the petty lord of some misbegotten muddy valley, realises the day is utterly lost. He does not wish to die with his men, so leaps onto his horse, and tries to ride clear of the bloody carnage. Will Draper sees. It was to be expected. The horse, thunders towards him, and he drops into a crouch. The whole bounty is there, within the one man, and to let him escape now will be disaster for them all.

The Welshman is carrying a heavy double edged axe, and will swing it with devastating effect at the Englishman, unless he jumps out of his path. Will waits until the charging man is almost on him, thrusts his blade up, and rolls to one side. The horses flying hooves miss crushing his skull by a hairs breadth. It gallops on for a few more yards, until the Welshman slides sideways, and falls to the snow covered ground. The Englishman's blade has taken him under the right armpit, and is still in place as he lands.

Will Draper runs towards his fallen enemy, switching his knife from left to right hand with practiced ease. The Welshman struggles to one knee, and pulls out the intrusive blade. If he can stand, he reasons, he can fight on.

The Englishman catches a handful of the man's long, matted hair, even as he tries to stand, draws the head back, and delivers a swift, killing blow into his throat. Owen Gryffid's blood gushes, warming his killer's clenched fist. Behind him, Will Draper knows, his surviving comrades are already stripping the corpses, stealing the better pairs of boots, and searching for any concealed coins.

"The horse is mine," he calls. The nearest man looks up from the body he is robbing, and assesses the Welsh Cob's value. In six long months, it is the most he has heard the quiet Englishman utter, other than a terse observation on the weather, or a brief opinion as to which trail to follow for the best. The Cob is sturdy, but not large enough to sell to some lord for using in the lists.

"Take it, Will, but what about the saddle bags?"

"I'll forgo my share of whatever they hold, John Morton," he replies, wiping his twin blades clean in the snow. "And I will undertake the trip to Ludlow for the bounty."

"Then I say you have a deal," John

Morton says, stunned at his friend's sudden loquacity. "Lodge our shares with Hal of Ludlow, the money changer who holds court by the cathedral. What say you, lads?"

The other four survivors all nod their approval. Will Draper is as honest a man as they could wish for, and he will do just as they ask of him, but no more. The sturdy horse will need to be fed, and it is not worth arguing about. Their comrade agrees to deliver the required proof, the severed head of Owen Gryffid, to the High Sheriff of Ludlow, as required, and receive the twenty pound bounty. He will leave their portions with Hal of Ludlow, who acts as an informal banker for the border shires, and then be on his way.

John Morton might miss the young man. They have served together in Ireland, and ridden bounty on a half dozen outlaws during the last six months, but Will wants to move on. England, he says, during a rare moment of discourse, is a large kingdom, and he wants to see more of it. The horse, Morton supposes, will make that possible.

"May that sturdy beast carry you far, Will," he says. The younger man sheaths his sword and slips the long, narrow bladed knife back into the straps on his wrist. It is

Spanish made, and cost him almost a month's wage in Dublin.

"Here, tie the proof up in his cloak," he suggests. "It's ruined with blood, and will not fetch any sort of price."

"May God be with you, brother," one of the other bounty men calls. Will acknowledges the sincerity of the man with a curt nod. He has as little time for God, as the creator of mankind has for him. If Will Draper had his way, their paths would never cross again.

*

As a youth of seventeen, he had prayed in the village church for the shaking sickness to leave his family be, and had watched, impotently, as first his mother, and then his brother and three sisters died. The new priest commended them all to God's good grace, after demanding payment of a fee. Without the priest's blessing, the man of God explained, his family would spend all eternity suffering the torments of purgatory.

Will Draper had already decided to leave the village. There was war in Ireland, he'd heard, and willing young men might do well to enlist in King Henry's gathering army. So he paid the priest with his last pennies, and had him mumble his badly flawed Latin cant over the newly dug graves.

The priest, a young man, was the bastard son of a nobleman in Yorkshire, who had been given the parish to keep him from under his father's feet. Even the lowest of the Baron's did not like to be reminded of their indiscretions, and a bought parish was a cheap option for a sinful lord's illegitimate offspring.

Father De Forest arrived in the village at the height of the fever, and had locked himself away in one of the church's cottages, with a woman he had picked up in Lincoln, and who he claimed as his housekeeper. God, Will thought, moves in mysterious ways.

In the night, he crept into the priest's house, cut his throat, and retrieved his money. Escape from Purgatory was not to be bought with a few coins, Will had decided.

He took the man's mule and, having heard that troops were embarking from the Welsh coast, he set off on a thirty mile journey through outlaw infested land. Will is a strong youth, and well armed, so concludes his journey without mishap.

He enlists without a problem. The king is not fussy these days, he is told. As long as you can use a sword, you are in. The sea is the worst part, churning and roaring until every man is sick to death. The boat, rat infested, and leaking like a sieve, gets them safely to port. Dublin is a shit hole, and the finest part of the forlorn country.

The Irish war proves to be little more than a lot of marching through fever infested bogs, and ruthless skirmishes with wild haired men, intent on strike and run tactics that infuriate the troops. It is Will who goes to his corporal, and suggests a clever ruse. The rebels never attack unless in superior force. He suggests sending out a dozen men on foot, to patrol the road west. A troop of horse must follow on, with stealth. It works, and a score of the Irish are killed in the first ambush, without a single English casualty.

Over and over, the trick works, with variations to keep the Irish wrong footed. Soon the men are deferring to Will Draper, relying on his good sense, and sharpness of wit. It is not long before the colonel of the regiment begins to hear very good reports of his new recruit, and sends for him.

Will's ability to read and write neatly astounds his commanding officer, who holds firmly to the belief that literacy is only for cunning priests, and clever lawyers. Gentlemen with noble connections have no need for such educated tricks.

"You don't look like much of a priest to me, boy," Colonel Foulkes says, once the strange thing is brought to his attention. "Damn me, but I wager your father was a man of law. God strike them all dead for their lawyer ways!"

"The old priest taught me," Will explains, referring to the mild old man who had served the village until his successor came, and had been like a grandfather to him, "He showed me how to write letters, and made me do my numbers. He used to say arithmetic was stronger than a cannon ball."

"Then you can keep accounts," the Colonel decides. "Sergeant at Arms, where the devil are you, man? Give this fellow a stripe and set him to work on the regimental accounts. The King will only pay for what I can prove. God save His Majesty, but he is beset by penny pinching men of law. This damned war is costing me dear, I fear. I shall not come out of it any the richer."

So it comes to pass that Will Draper is the regimental clerk. He sits down with a great ledger, and begins to unravel the cipher-like scrawls of officers demands for new boots, fresh arms and horses. After a few hours, it begins to make sense, and he is able to draw up a rough, but accurate set of single entry accounts. By the second day, he has worked out a way of making the regiment a nice profit. It is almost legal.

"It's the horses, sir," he explains, pointing to a long column of figures. The Colonel nods sagely, unable to comprehend the neatly drawn up entries. "A chit comes in, requesting fresh mounts. We buy them, and issue them as required."

"Is this important, Corporal Draper?" Colonel Foulkes asks the eager young man. "My dinner, for what it's worth, is growing cold."

"We should appoint a single agent to buy horses, sir," Will Draper explains. "He will buy them at say, two pounds a piece, and sell them on to the regiment at fifty shillings a head. You then bill the crown for them at fifty shillings, and our agent returns eight shillings to us. He makes two shillings per horse, and we make eight shillings. The King, God save him, can pay fifty shillings, I'm sure."

"Dear God, but I ought to hang you

for such an outrageous suggestion, Draper. Will it work?"

"With all sorts of things, sir," Will replies. "Providing the papers exist to show the purchase, it is all quite legal. We could do it with fodder, boots for the men, and general rations."

"How much would this make… for the regiment?"

"Perhaps fifty pounds a month."

"Free and clear?"

"As the wind, sir." Will closes his ledger with a snap. He senses that a deal has been done. "I trust you will take the extra funds into your safe keeping?"

"Of course." Colonel Foulkes is not quick witted, and he must think it through for a moment. At last, he speaks again. "And what about you, Will Draper? How can I trust you?"

"That's easy enough, Colonel.," Will replies. "Make me the regimental procurement agent."

"Why?"

"Because my one fifth part will allow me to support my new rank."

"A new rank, corporal?"

"Yes, sir. A regimental procurement officer must have a more suitable rank.

Something substantial, I think. Captain would do well enough."

"Get out," Foulkes growls, but it turns into a chuckle. "I shall expect to see you but once a month. Is that fully understood… Captain Draper?"

Will bows, and leaves the tent. He has much work to do, and the regiment is in sore need of supplies.

*

Three years in Ireland make Will Draper into a hard, capable fighting man; a man of some considerable fortune. By the time he is twenty one, he had amassed over four hundred pounds, and is ready to lead the life of a country gentleman. The money, he reasons, wisely invested with the Lombard banker, Arturo Galti, in the city of Chester, should bring in enough for him to keep a fine house, and a hundred acres of good sheep land. It is more than he could ever have hoped for, yet the idea of such a life leaves him feeling unfulfilled.

Will Draper resigns his commission, bids his friends farewell, and returns to England. The Irish Sea is as unforgiving as ever, and the small cog which flits between

Dublin and Anglesey is forced of course, and takes in water to the point where even the captain of the craft starts to pray. After a bad day and night, they manage to land safely, and Will swears never to travel by sea again.

His arrival in Chester is equally inauspicious. Will Draper finds the banking house of Arturo Galti closed, with boards nailed up at all of the windows. A vague disquiet invades his heart, and he is forced to inquire with a neighbour. He knocks on the door of the elegant town house until he hears someone coming, and grumbling at being disturbed.

He introduces himself to the stout master of the house, and asks after the Galti banking family. The man, a very prosperous weaver by trade, looks Will Draper up and down, as if examining a bolt of decent quality Flemish linen.

"They've gone," he explains, at length. "These three weeks past, it was. They shut up shop one night, as usual, and were away by the morning. I doubt you will find Galti, or any Lombard still within England, Captain Draper."

"Where have they gone?" Will asks, maintaining a calm facade.

"Did you have much lodged with

them?" the man asks, by way of answer. "A few poor souls have come calling."

"All my earnings from the Irish wars," Will Draper is driven to confess. "I have scarcely enough to buy food and lodging for a few nights. I must find them, and recover my gold."

"Do you know Italy well, then?"

"You taunt me, Master Weaver!"

"I speak good sense," the man insists. "They have fled, under the King's great displeasure, and will not stop until they are safe in France or Italy. The Galtis and their fellow Lombards failed to understand about His Majesty's great problem."

"What do you mean?" Will demands to know. "I have been away too long to understand what you say."

"The King has no son. He wants one, and the talk is of him putting aside Queen Katherine. The Pope and his church will have none of it, of course."

"And how does that affect my hard earned gold, sir?" Will Draper sees that the king's actions have robbed him of his fortune, and he is seething with rage.

"Henry needs money to pay his army, and to buy jewels for his filthy trollops," the weaver continues. "The Lombards were to make him a large loan, but then Pope Clement has forbade them. They were in a cleft stick, you see. The King demanded one thing, and then the Pope demanded otherwise. So, they plotted amongst themselves, and fled in the night. Poor Henry will not get his loan, and you will not see your money, until the Galti family are free to return. I know Master Galti well, young man, and he is a most honourable fellow. Be assured, the fellow will invest your gold well, and someday, return it to you much enhanced."

"Someday?" Will Draper curses under his breath. He has nothing but his broken down old horse, a change of doublet, a few shillings in his purse, and no prospect of seeing his fortune for many years. "The king has done me a bad turn, sir, and I am at a loss as to how I can proceed."

"You will want work in the meantime, I suppose?" the man asks.

"I am not a weaver, sir," Will tells him, smiling, and tapping the hilt of his sword. "Do you have any work for a battle hardened soldier?"

"By God, Captain Draper… but I do believe I have," the weaver says, with sudden inspiration. "I know just how best you might be employed... and it will benefit us both, I think."

"Then speak up, sir," Will says, "for you are my best hope at the moment."

The weaver explains how King Henry's bounty works, and makes the young soldier an interesting offer. He can equip and fund Will Draper as a bounty man, in return for a part share in his takings.

"Chasing the Welsh, surely, can be no harder than chasing after the Irish," Will Draper concludes, with a rather simple soldier's logic. "Though such work cannot be done alone. I must find men to serve with me. Can I rely on you to find them some decent weapons, horses, and rations ... enough to feed us for about a month?"

"A single month?" The rich weaver asks, surprised at so modest a request. "Why only a month, young fellow?"

"Because, after that time, we will be either self sufficient ... or dead, sir."

*

Two days later, the young soldier of fortune is back aboard his familiar cog, and heading for Dublin. Once back in Ireland, he goes to his old colonel's regiment, where he recruit's almost a half company of willing men, ready to make their fortunes gathering in bounty.

Now, seven months later, and with almost nine pounds in his purse, Will Draper is finally done with hunting outlaws, and sets out to see England. Nine pounds is not the fortune he expected, but it will keep him alive, whilst he seeks out some adventure where he might make a goodly living.

He had heard wonderful tales about London, and other great towns, such as Nottingham and Leicester. It is a toss of the coin at a crossroads that sent him on his way towards the latter place and introduces him to a future he could never have guessed at.

2   The Cardinal's Messenger

The sturdy Welsh Cob has earned herself a rest. She has carried Will Draper for two days, and for the best part of seventy miles, until he is almost within sight of Leicester. He slides from the saddle, and leads the horse for a little while, allowing her time to regain its wind. There is, in his mind, no particular cause to hurry, other than to be under cover before darkness falls.

The horse's ears prick up, even as Will Draper senses the subtle change, himself. In the far distance, wheeling crows, and clouds of dust foretell the approach of a large body of men. Over a hundred, he guesses, all mounted, but coming on very slowly. This represents a formidable force, and Will wonders what is afoot.

An army marching to Leicester? Has he missed some vital piece of information, and is he now riding into a war? Henry is at war, perhaps, but with whom? Have the Spanish crept ashore, or the French landed? He has never met either, but will fight anyone, if the money is right. Idly, he wonders how the foreigners fight. Three horsemen appear on the brow of a low hill, pause, then began to gallop towards him. His

Welsh Cob stands stock still, and blows air from her nostrils. She scents danger, and is bracing herself for a charge, once her new master commands.

Three mounted men, Will sees. The leading one has drawn his sword, and spurs his horse on, racing ahead of his comrades. Had Will wanted, he might have told the man not to be so impetuous. He might also have told him not to allow a potential enemy to get on his blind side. But Will did not want. The advantage is his, he sees, and he is quite content with that.

"In the King's name!" the first horseman shouts. He reigns in, sharply, with Will Draper standing, casually to his left. Further most away from the swing of your sword arm, he thinks. Now I am in charge.

"Which King would that be?" Will asks.

"You impudent…" The words are cut off as, grasping the man's left boot, Will levers him from his saddle. He hit's the ground hard, and his companions begin to laugh. There will be no killing today. Unless the young fool on the ground has other ideas.

"I'm just a traveller, sir," he says, but the young man, made to look foolish, is intent on dangerously compounding his folly. He curses, and unsheathes a fine, light rapier, unfit for the purpose of killing an enemy. Will is forced to draw his own sword and, with two or three swift moves, he disarms his attacker and aims the point at the young fellow's throat. "Enough, good sir, I have no wish to kill a stranger ... It might cause ill feeling."

The man looks into Will's eyes, and sees that here is a man who can do as he promises. He looks to his two friends, who shake their heads at him. Do not be foolish, the looks say. It is not their fight. They have been sent, merely to see who this stranger is. The older of the three dismounts, and holds out a hand for Will to grasp. He is of an altogether different sort, Will thinks. Cross this one, and you will find yourself in a desperate fight. He is lean, and has the look of a killing man about him.

"Might I name myself, my young ruffian. I am Sir Andrew Jennings, and these useless louts, are two of my men. And you, sir?"

"Captain Will Draper, late of the King's army in Ireland." He neglects to mention his time roaming Welsh hills, in search of elusive brigands. These men are gentlemen, and might not appreciate his choice of career, he thinks.

"A soldier, young Harry," Andrew Jennings says to his defeated comrade. "There is no shame in being bested by a battle seasoned soldier, is there? Come, shake hands on it, like gentlemen!"

Will and Harry shake hands, and he marvels at how easily he has become a gentleman in this company. All it takes is to pitch a fool from his horse, and knock aside his sword. Jennings it turns out, works for the Duke of Northumberland, and is commander of a troop of gentlemen, sent by King Henry, to escort the cardinal back to London.

"A Cardinal needs a hundred men to protect him?" Will asks, and is told the story by Harry Cork, who now wishes to be his best friend.

"The Cardinal is Thomas Wolsey. He has failed the King in the matter of his annulment from Katherine, and is to face serious charges, once back in London," young Harry explains.

"He has been in the north of Yorkshire, fomenting much trouble for His Majesty," Jennings sneers. "We are not here to protect the scoundrel, but take him back to face charges."

Powerful men have been whispering in Henry's ear, accusing the Cardinal of treason. The King is in a quandary, for he loves no man more than Thomas Wolsey, but does not wish to upset the powerful Duke of Norfolk and his niece, Anne Boleyn. So the King shows his apparent displeasure, by ordering the dear old Cardinal's arrest.

It is believed by all at court that Henry will huff and puff, before embracing Wolsey, and forgiving him for his sins. Wolsey will rend his clothes in anguish, swear his devotion to the king, and bestow his much valued blessing. Some valuable land and money will change hands, and Cardinal Wolsey will regain his seat at the King's right hand, suitably chastised by his benevolent master. A squall over nothing, those in the know mutter, between two powerful men. That is all.

The Cardinal, in the meantime, is under close arrest, and being escorted back to face Henry's wrath, Harry Cork explains.

"The long term result... the king's forgiveness... is a foregone conclusion," he says. "Though the Lady Anne would not, had she her way, suffer him to live another month."

"Lady Anne?"

"Anne Boleyn," Sir Andrew Jennings tells him. "One of the powerful Howard clan. A niece to the Duke of Norfolk. She is the King's new… lady, and would be far more. She will be Queen."

"I wager the church is not happy about that," Will says, as he mounts his Cob. "Priests always look after their own. This cardinal will find a way out of the difficulty, one way or another."

"We shall lodge at Leicester Abbey tonight," young Harry tells him. "Join with us, Will. The King ever has need of good men."

"A tempting offer, Harry," Will replies. From bounty man to king's man, in one easy step. "Perhaps I might find time to teach you how to fence?"

"Most kind of you," Harry rejoins. "And perhaps I can teach you how to dress like a gentleman, rather than a Welsh sheep farmer?"

"My woollen jerkin keeps out this November chill, sir," Will says, as he spurs his horse into a gentle gallop.

*

There is little free space at the abbey,

and many of the escorting party are forced to seek rooms in nearby villages, or ride on into Leicester. Will always carries his bed about with him, and unfurls it in the hayloft of the abbey's stable. The home spun blanket over an armful of straw suffices. His sleep is always a light one, thanks to his time on campaign, and his bad conscience. Sometimes, but not too often, the face of the priest comes to him, and he awakens with a start. Other times he sees his mother, and has to stifle a tear.

Tonight is different. The armed men, when they come, have burning brands, and are shouting out his name. Will rolls out of his makeshift bed and runs for open country. He is barely a dozen paces from the barn when an excited shout goes up, and there are armed men all about him. For a moment, he thinks to draw his dagger, and take a few of them with him, but they are not threatening him with weapons, and seem happy to have found him. One of Jennings' men slaps him on the back, and makes a course jest about finding him sleeping with animals in the barn. So he smiles at them and has no other recourse than to let them take him wherever they might wish.

They troop along, marching him into

the gloomy confines of the magnificent abbey, and place him in a small, tapestry lined room without benefit of any windows. There is a small niche in one wall, and a silver crucifix is its only adornment. Will doubts he can get away without doing murder, and wonders what calamity has befallen him. Fate is a funny thing, and it only now, when he is at his most vulnerable, that providence deals him a winning hand.

Sir Andrew Jennings comes in then, bowing and showing in a big, dangerous looking man. Will Draper gages his height and weight, as he would a horse, and wonders if he might have to kill him with a dagger thrust, and flee. He can think of no crime they might know of, but his conscience is ever flawed with guilt of some sort or other. So he waits, and listens to his fate.

"Will Draper, a captain in the King's service," Sir Andrew says, naming Will to the fur clad giant. "I have the honour to present Henry Percy, the Earl of Northumberland." Will has just enough sense to bow, and kiss the proffered ring hand. The big man smiles, and seems benign enough, so Will leaves his concealed dagger where it is.

"My Lord," he says. The shadow of death has receded. Harry Percy is a grand Duke of the Realm, Will reasons, and surely does not do his own murder. "How may I be of service?"

"Tell him, Jennings," Percy snaps. "I want my bed!"

"Cardinal Wolsey is…"

"Bishop…" Percy says, vindictively. The cardinal is reduced in rank, by order of the courts of justice, and Harry Percy, once humiliated by him, and an unforgiving enemy, must have his pound of flesh.

"Er.. Yes… Bishop Wolsey is dead, Captain Draper."

"My condolences," Will says, waiting for the part he has been chosen to play. "I dare say many will be pleased."

"Pleased? God's teeth, but the damnable bastard has cheated us all at the last!" Percy roared. "Do you not see? He has died in his bloody sleep. There can be no public trial. No reckoning of accounts against him. Who will be able to unravel his affairs? Henry will be furious… but he must be told. Yes, we must send a messenger at once, no matter the danger."

Will sighs. There is to be no sleep for him tonight then. The fine gentlemen are obviously frightened that the King will dismember the bearer of such news. And well he might. As a small child, he was told the tale of how the Tudors would eat children for supper … right down to the smallest bone.

"It is a hard ride, over dangerous roads, My Lord," Will says, opening the negotiations.

"Then, God's Speed to you, Captain Draper. Jennings, give him a purse of money, and the message in writing. Damn and blast this to Hell and back, but we will need a priest, or a clerk of the law. Go and me find one who can scrawl the words down!"

"I can write, My Lord," Will confesses.

"By the holy bollocks of Christ!" Percy roars. He is much wont to such vulgarities, thinking it makes him more fearsome, and can curse better than a Venetian sailor. In reality, it makes him sound like a spoiled child. "Do it, man!" he says to Sir Andrew, and hands him a ring.

The carved impression of the onyx ring will be the messages authenticator, and prove that it came from Northumberland himself. The King will know that Wolsey is dead, and can then tell who he wishes to tell.

Will shall take the message, and a small bag of coins for his troubles, and go to London. The old priest told him once, how bearers of bad news were once killed for their trouble, and he sighs again.

He is given parchment, ink and a quill. Sir Andrew dictates the news tersely. To His Highness, the most noble…. etcetera, he begins and concludes with a simple phrase. Bishop Wolsey is dead, this 29th day of November, 1530. Will scratches away slowly, using his best hand. At the foot of the page, he adds, *'I commend this messenger to you as a fine and loyal subject'*. Sir Andrew sprinkles sawdust on the letter, and blows it dry. He is either a gentleman, and cannot read a word, or too disinterested to check the wording.

"Try first at York Place, the Cardinal's old palace, then the Palace of Westminster next," he advises. Then he watches as Will melts the candle wax, drips it onto the folded letter, and presses the ring down, sealing it against prying eyes.

But Will's eyes have already pried. His audacious addendum might bring him advancement, or death. He fears neither, but has a preference in the matter. His Welsh Cob is fully rested, and there will be a fresh mount waiting at Harrow, should he have need. He mounts, and is leaving by the south facing gate, when Harry Cork, his new found friend catches at his bridle and beckons him to lean forward in the saddle for a whispered message.

"For your own sake, and if you are my friend …go first to the house of Thomas Cromwell at Austin Friars," Harry says. "He will reward you well for this terrible news. If he asks, tell him Harry Cork sent you, and begs that he is remembered kindly, if some post should ever open in his household."

"Cromwell you say?" The young soldier of fortune nods, and the two men clasp hands. "Very well, I shall heed your words, Harry."

"Then go with God, Will," his friend says, and slaps the horse on her rump. Will Draper rides out through the courtyard gate and urges his Welsh Cob into a steady gallop.

*

The winter roads are bad and, in some places they are almost non-existent. It will take him the rest of the night, and most of the next day to reach London. There he must choose whether to call on Thomas Cromwell, as advised, or go directly to the King, as commanded by the Duke of Northumberland.

Will has been out of the country a while, but has some knowledge of things. Cromwell, he knows, is a lawyer, and also the cardinal's most respected man. The cardinal is dead. If Cromwell has lost his protecting master, it might be dangerous to be seen with him. It is the very idea of riding into danger that finally decides him.

He will seek out Thomas Cromwell, deliver his news, then ride on to the King, where he will hand over a letter with an unbroken seal. With any luck, there might be two rewards on offer. Besides, a good lawyer might be able to help him track down his vanished gold. Four hundred and seventeen pounds, sitting in a French or Milanese bank is of little use to him.

He keeps to a steady pace, never demanding too much from the sturdy Cob, and reaches London just as darkness is falling. He asks his way often, and finds himself outside an imposing house situated on the land once owned by the venerable friars of Austin. The land is still occupied by Augustinian friars, and one, swaddled in a heavy black cloak is lighting torches at the gate. The firebrands illuminate a strange scene of beggars, and waifs, and the friar waves to them.

"Go around to the kitchens, my friends," he tells them. "There is hot soup and bread waiting for you. Those without a bed may sleep in the stables tonight."

Will Draper is tired, but knows that civility will work better with this man rather than making demands. He slips from the saddle and removes his sodden bonnet.

"Good fellow," he starts. The man shuffles about and squints at him in the flickering light. "I seek the house of Master Thomas Cromwell. Have I found it, brother?"

"Yes, master," the stout, middle aged retainer says. "Are you seeking shelter and food for the night, or have you some sort of business with him?"

"*With him*, yes," Will Draper says, pointedly. The message is for Thomas Cromwell's ears alone. "My name is Captain Will Draper, and I would speak with your master, most urgently. It concerns Cardinal Wolsey."

"Please, go to the house. I will see your horse is attended to," the man says, snatching the reigns from Will's tired grasp. He goes inside, and is amazed at the splendour of the interior. There are coats of arms painted upon the walls, and doors leading off in all directions. Before him is a great, wooden staircase. A greyhound is lounging at its foot, and looks him over with scant interest.

Will has never been in a house with more than one real floor before, and the beauty of the well lit entrance hall makes him understand what true wealth really is. Thomas Cromwell is, for the moment, a great man… or at least, a rich one.

The servant comes shuffling back in, and throws off his black cloak. A young boy runs to catch it, bowing. The old servant is, in fact, Thomas Cromwell, and the small jest has enlivened what promised to be a dull evening spent reading by the fire.

The middle aged lawyer examines the young man, sees the sword, and notes the face. He is good with faces, and sums this one up. The face of a most dangerous man. He mutters it, but in Latin. His bland expression never slips.

"*Mea Culpa,*" Will Draper responds to the words.

"You have Latin?" Cromwell asks.

"Some." Will recalls the lessons, given by the old priest, and sees now how they are to help him in the wider world. "*Et ego um vobis*, My Lord."

"A most scholarly soldier... however it is not *um,* but *in ... in vobis*. That is to say that you *... come to serve me*. In what way, I wonder, young man?" Cromwell says, ushering Will into a book lined room which has a roaring fire in the grate. "Come in to my library and warm yourself by the hearth. Have you a bed for the night? No, stupid of me to ask. You have ridden hard, all the way from the Cardinal, God bless and save his good soul. How is he?"

"Alas, sir... but it is not good news," Will says. He takes a deep breath before saying: "Cardinal Wolsey is dead."

"Oh, sweet Christ... what... how...?"

Will Draper recites the contents of the dictated letter, from memory. Thomas Cromwell turns to face the fire. The flames light his face up, making him look like a satanic being, fresh from one of Hell's deeper pits. He stares, unblinking, into the flames, then speaks.

"They called him '*bishop*'?"

"They did, sir. Harry Percy insisted

on it."

"Only the Pope can bring down an anointed cardinal," Cromwell mutters. "I believe Percy and the rest have over stepped their authority in this matter."

"I am sorry to bring you so sad a message," Will tells him, wondering what he should do now. The news is clearly not to Master Cromwell's taste, and his grief is obvious.

"My servants will make a room up for you, Captain Draper," the lawyer says, as if reading his mind. "You can deliver your message to the King tomorrow. Hand it to one of his gentlemen, and try not to give your name. It will do you no good to be remembered as the man who brought this message. Instead, you will return here, to me. Is that understood?"

"Am I to be your man then, sir?" Will Draper asks.

"Do you wish that?"

"I do." The words came out without a thought. Will's instinct has taken command. Thomas Cromwell is his sort of man, and promises to be a good master.

"Then you will become my own creature, Will," Cromwell tells him. "They will tell you tales about me. Of how I am the son of a blacksmith, and have served the cardinal too well. They will tell you I have some blood on my hands, and that I hate God. What say you to that?"

"They used to tell me that the Tudors ate children, my lord," Will replies. "I am quite able to make up my own mind about you."

"And if I turn out to be a baby eater?"

"That is between you, and your God."

"*My* God, Will?" Cromwell studies him. "Is yours different than mine, or … is it something else you mean?"

"God has his place, sir," Will said. "I nod to him, when I must, but am ever a practical man."

"Martin Luther is a practical man," Cromwell replied. "If your mind is that way set, it must never interfere with the running of my household. Understood?"

"Yes, sir. May I ask a question?"

"Ask it, Captain."

"Who is Martin Luther?"

Cromwell laughs then. He has not laughed since the last time he saw his master, Cardinal Wolsey. Now, here is a young man to tell him that the greatest of men is dead. Alone and untended, in a crumbling old monastery. I should have been with him, the lawyer thinks, allowing sentiment to cloud good judgement.

"Never mind, Will. How did you come to find out the contents of Percy's letter so precisely?"

"I wrote it, sir," Will replies. "They could not, and I am well read, and can write with a goodly hand."

"Was your father a gentleman then?"

"I don't know. He died when I was a small, edible child, sir."

"You have a quick tongue, and an even quicker wit," Cromwell decides. "You shall be my confidential agent. How does twelve pounds a year sound?"

"I have my own fortune, Master Cromwell," Will says, and tells the lawyer of his recent misfortune. All the while the older man smiles and nods his understanding of the younger man's plight.

"Your weaver told you the truth, Will," he says. "King Henry is ever short of ready money, and turned to the Lombards for a loan. The branches in Rome, Milan and Naples are loyal to the Pope, and the Holy Roman Emperor. They stalled over making a decision... then quibbled over interest rates.

The King is not a patient sort, and he became much too insistent. The French and Italian offices refused to lend, and the English Lombards melted away. Fearing, no doubt, that His Majesty would seek some form of retribution."

"Then I have the King to blame," Will Draper says. "You are a lawyer, sir. Can the King be taken to law? How should I proceed?"

"Patience, Will," Cromwell replies. In one short hour he has evaluated the young soldier, and finds him to be most suitable for his purposes. Apart from that, Cromwell has a single flaw. He likes, for no apparent reason, certain people, and his friendship, once given, is firm and unwavering. He has been Cardinal Wolsey's friend and loyal servant for many years, and will not drop him now, even in death. "Serve me well, and I will write to my friends in Florence, asking them to re-establish access to your fortune."

"My sword is yours, sir." Draper bows, then adds: "For twelve pounds a year."

"I am more covetous of your mind," Cromwell says. "It is young, and eager to learn. You will become one of my young men. I have Richard and Rafe, who are my known men, and help me with my daily legal work.. You will be my *unknown* man. A silent shadow, flitting about the place, sorting out things that are best not committed to writing."

Cromwell's domestic arrangements are complicated. Richard Cromwell is eighteen, and a nephew who has recently taken his name as a sign of respect, and Ralph Sadler is twenty one, and a foundling, of sorts. He is *Rafe* to all, and Thomas Cromwell often plays cleverly on the pronunciation, saying tow for tough, or saying the young man is 'a *rough* about my neck'. His friends laugh so politely that he thinks he must come up with better jests.

"You wish me to kill for you?" Will is testing the waters, to see how much of his soul this affable old devil wants.

"Is it so hard a matter?" Cromwell asks. In his younger days, he fought for the French King in Italy, and sometimes killed men.

"Not in the heat of battle," Will concedes.

"Then it is not a sin to kill for one's country?" Cromwell asks.

"You really do speak like a lawyer, sir," Will responds. "Perhaps we should take each day as it comes. Bid me do this, or that, as you wish, and I will see what my poor conscience says."

"Well enough said," Thomas Cromwell tells him. The Captain is young for such a position, but in a nation where half the people are, because of poverty and pestilence, under the age of twenty, a man must mature quickly if he is to get on. "We shall do nicely for one another, my friend… rest easy."

A bed is warmed with hot cinders, and a small fire lit in his chamber. Will Draper is now a shadowy part of the Austin Friars household. Cromwell is a good host, and lights his new man to his allotted room, leading the way with a tall tallow candle. He pushes back the door, and chases away the pretty young girl who has just finished with her warming pan.

"They really told you to write that?" he asks Will Draper, one last time. "They actually called him '*bishop*?'" He tut tuts beneath his breath, and ushers Will into his room. "We rise early in Austin Friars. With the first cock crow, my friend!"

Will crosses to the bed and, exhausted from the long ride, he falls into it. He feels as though he has come home. In a matter of moments he is in a deep sleep, untroubled by leering priests, conniving lords, or a sad faced mother. His new master stands outside the chamber for a few moments, until he hears the sound of gentle snoring, then makes his way back down the wide staircase, and the comforting surrounds of his library.

*

Thomas Cromwell seldom sleeps more than a few hours each night, and thinks slumber is a thief of life. He has the work of two men to do, and so needs the stolen night time hours. He returns to his warm book lined study, and lifts down two slender, leather bound books from a high shelf. Each bears a title. One says *'Amicis Gloriosum'*, and the other *'Vindicatio'*. He turns to the first page of the book of vengeance, reads the name and details thereon, and smiles to himself. Then he turns a dozen leaves, to the next empty page, takes up his quill, and writes. His letters are neatly formed, and written as beautifully as any monk or priest might manage. Not bad for a drunken blacksmith's son, he thinks.

The slender volume bears the names

of enemies, both dead and living, and is much consulted these days. Thomas Cromwell feels the emptiness of loss, and wonders how he can continue without the benevolent support of his own dear cardinal. He fights down his tears, and marvels at how savage great men can be.

"Oh, Wolsey," he mutters," how could you let them bring you to this? How could you keep faith with so variable a king? Those bastards called you 'bishop', My Lord… and must pay the price.

He carefully writes down the one name, *Harry Percy, 6ᵗʰ Earl of Northumberland.* Next to this he writes ' *Canis reddam'* and underscores it twice. The dog will pay. Then he makes a note of all he knows about Percy, and writes down just how he will make this particular dog howl. It is well past midnight, but when he rings the small bell by his elbow, Rafe Sadler appears at once.

"Still up, Rafe?"

"Yes, sir. I have a brief to complete," Rafe replies. In fact, he never retires until Cromwell does, and he lingers in the next office, waiting for just such a summons. "How can I help you?"

"Cardinal Wolsey is dead."

"Yes, I heard," Rafe replies. "Norfolk will be angry at missing an execution. Did he suffer?"

"From a broken heart, I think," Cromwell says. "He always believed the king would forgive him. Though what his crimes were... I do not know. We have a guest. Captain Will Draper is his name. On the morrow send our agents out to find out what they can of the fellow. See he is well fed, and escorted to the royal court."

"His life might be in danger," Rafe says. "The king is bound to be furious at Wolsey's death. I think he meant to break him... then forgive him, but only after stripping him of his church treasure and land. Now he has no accomplished minister to consult... other than that rogue Norfolk."

"And the Duke of Suffolk," Cromwell says. "Charles Brandon is not a clever man, but he is the king's best friend, and his words carry much weight. If we are to survive these turbulent times, we must win over one or the other to our side."

"Norfolk serves no man," says Rafe.

"Then let us look to Suffolk," Cromwell decides. "We have come too far to let it all go now, my boy."

"What of Percy?"

"Percy has gone too far," Cromwell says, patting his *Vindicatio*. "I fear the time has come to act against him."

3   The King's Jew

Will Draper wakes to find a suit of clothes laid out for him at the foot of the bed. This worries him greatly. That someone could enter his room, and not disturb him, is personally dangerous. The next time, they might come with a knife, or a deadly efficient garrotte, rather than a fine doublet and hose.

He dresses, and admires the well cut jacket, with its slightly puffed sleeves and fine embroidery. On the sleeve the letter C has been picked out in gold thread. The black Worsted suit, and the unobtrusive 'C', marks him down as one of Master Cromwell's men. He is dressed like a wealthy lawyer's clerk, and it makes him smile. Clothes, indeed, really do maketh the man.

The sword, when it is buckled on, will, perhaps, make him look slightly more sinister. It is double-edged, and has a distinctly foreign look to it. The sturdy iron hand-guard is in a figure-of-eight loop, and there is a small, gilded shield on the hilt, adorned with a silver cross. The yard long blade has three shallow fullers running along most of its length, to help the blood and gore flow away easily. The second small shield on the reverse of the grip is engraved with an angry looking bird. Colonel Foulkes once told him that it is the Imperial Eagle of Germany, and the Holy Roman Empire. Taken from the dead body of a minor Irish lord, its origin will remain, for ever, a mystery.

The overall impression is that you should be afraid of him, but not quite know why. He goes down the steeply pitched stairs and is directed by a small child to the kitchens, where a half dozen young men are already sitting, eating their breakfast.

"Master Draper," one of the men says, as he points to an empty stretch of bench. "You are just in time. There is thick cut bacon, fresh sheep kidneys, grilled livers, eggs, bread and hard cheese. What is your fancy?"

"My rank is captain, sir... but all here may call me Will." He can smell the meat and offal as it is being fried, just a few feet away and recalls that he has not eaten hot food for almost three days. He resists the urge to stuff himself full, unsure as to what the coming day will throw at him. Instead, he takes some fresh baked bread, and a thick slice of creamy yellow cheese.

"It is Flemish," another says. "They make fine cheese in the Netherlands, Will. My master says you have a message to deliver this morning, and for me to show you the way. The King is down river, visiting his current lady, but will be back at noon."

"I am like a good hunting dog," Will says. "Point me in the right direction, and let me off the leash."

This amuses the company, and they laugh and slap the table in appreciation. Will Draper is Thomas Cromwell's faithful dog, they say, but what breed would he wish to be?

"An Irish Wolfhound," Will replies, recognising their spirited good humour. There is no malice in this room. They are all in the same boat, and if their master ever falls from grace, they will sink or swim together. "I spent some years in Ireland, and much admired their ability to run down their prey."

Thomas Cromwell is suddenly amongst them, adjusting the folds of his black lawyer's robe. No one has heard his approach, and the young men jostle to make room at the table for him. He bows his head, murmurs a brief prayer, and reaches for a fat blood sausage.

"I care little what breed of dog you are, Master Draper, as long as you have a strong bite. Have you eaten yet? I see the suit fits. I guessed you to be the same size as Rafe." He nods to one of the young men. He is slightly older than the rest, and has a strong looking face. Will nods his thanks, and bites into his bread.

"Deliver your despatch, and come back to me, Will," Cromwell mutters to him. The others play deaf. Their master has a new conscript, and will be busy with him for a while. There are things, secret things, to impart, and Thomas Cromwell is not the sort to delegate so important a task to a lesser man than he. "There is a delicate mission I want you to undertake."

One of the young men hears this. He frowns, and makes as if to speak. Cromwell raises two fingers, effectively stilling his voice. Richard Cromwell accepts his uncle's unspoken decision, and subsides back into his place. He stabs at his food, and transports a thick chunk of pork to his grease stained mouth. He is a huge man, and can eat twice the amount of any other present.

"I'll be back as soon as I can, sir." Will has never visited London before, and has a sketchy idea of how things work. "Is my horse being readied for the journey?"

"That is not necessary," Rafe Sadler says. Thomas Cromwell advises him to take a boat from London Bridge, upstream. The couple of pennies will be money well spent.

"The city is congested, and a fleet footed man can go where a horse may not pass," Cromwell tells him. "Take Barnaby Fowler with you. He knows the streets, and can help avoid the stews and bawdy houses."

Will tries to object, but is overruled. It is only later that he realises why Barnaby is there. Thomas Cromwell is a lawyer, and seldom takes any man's word at face value. Barnaby Fowler is to accompany the new man, not as a guide, but as a witness to the morning's events.

Breakfast passes with a flurry of exchanges between master and men. Rafe is for the courts, to fetch some documents, Richard must ride to Putney to collect some rents. Another is detailed to attend on the new harbour master at Tilbury. Even Cromwell's son, young Gregory, home from school for the approaching Christmas festivities, is given a task to keep him occupied. He is to exercise the household's greyhounds on the heath, and help his comrades about the great house.

It has snowed a little during the night, and the edges of the wide river are frosted with ice. They stroll the half mile from Austin Friars, down towards the bridge. Will and Barnaby Fowler are seemingly out of luck. There is not a boat to be had, save one that has already been hailed by an elderly gentleman and his two young companions. The boatman ships oars and steps into the shallows, ready to help his passengers aboard.

He stops, as if suddenly struck by a thunderbolt, then begins to cross himself with the right hand, and wave away the old man with the left. The old man protests and, beckoning to the girl and young man with him, attempts to approach the boat. The river man swears wickedly, and raises his oar, as if to strike out at them. The younger fellow raises an arm in defence, and conjures a dagger from his open doublet.

Will has seen enough. The men might well be able to fend for themselves, but the woman, he sees, is young, and very pretty. He approaches, and asks if he might be of service. The old man turns to him, with a surprised look on his face.

"We seek only to take a boat up river, sir," he says, gesturing to the aggressive boatman. "This rogue is refusing us passage, and threatens us with violence."

"You can walk for all I care, you old bastard," the man growls at him. "I'll not hire out to you, or any of your sort."

"We wish to go the same way," Will says, calmly. Barnaby comes up beside him, and pulls at his sleeve. He wants his new comrade to come away. There is hidden danger here that is new friend does not perceive. Will shrugs him off. "Would you refuse me passage, master boatman?"

The man sees the cut of the new man, and the handy way he wears his sword. It hangs, ready for use, rather than dangles in a more fashionable way. Then he looks into his hard eyes, and casts his own down.

"Begging your pardon, master, but I will take you and your companion to wherever you command," he says, "for that is what my licence demands of me."

"Then it is I who shall hire you, good fellow. These three people are with me. Help them aboard." The man frowns at this sudden turn of events. He is caught out, and has not the wits to simply bow and keep his mouth shut.

"They are Christ killers, sir," he complains. "God tells us that we should not suffer them to live."

"Really?" He turns to Barnaby Fowler. "Come now, my clever friend. You are a man trained in the law. Can you not guide us in this matter?"

Barnaby is a Cromwell man, which makes him one of the best trained legal minds in London. He sees Will is determined to win the day, no matter what, and considers the matter.

"Sir, might I beg of you your name?" he asks.

"My name is Isaac ben Mordecai, of Toledo," the old man responds. "These are my late son's children, Moshe and Miriam."

"I see. May I ask if this man's claim is correct?" Barnaby draws himself up to his full height, and places a regal hand on his heart. "Did you, sir, by your very own hand, murder Our Lord, Jesus Christ?"

"I did not," the old Jew replies, smiling. "Even I am not that old!"

"There now, boatman, this poor gentleman bears no guilt in the business," Barnaby says, climbing into the craft. He half expects an oar to come crashing down onto his unguarded head. "These people have a watertight alibi. Now, might I suggest you put your oars to their proper use, before my impetuous friend draws his blade. He is a mad Irishman who lives for adventure, and has done murder already this week."

Will touches the hilt of his sword, and the man returns to his oars, his face burning with anger. He is a river man, born stubborn, and must play a final card. His licence only allows for four passengers, he tells them , and they number five. Barnaby sighs and opens his purse.

"We shall count the young girl as baggage," he says, "and pay the extra penny." The matter is resolved with a tiny bribe. Will Draper would have done it differently, and the boatman would have come off far the worse for it. He holds out his hand and steadies first the old man, and then his pretty granddaughter as they board. The young Moshe jumps aboard, slips his dagger out of sight, and seats himself directly opposite the rower, glowering at him. For two farthings, he would cut his throat and throw his body into the river.

"You are from Toledo," Will says. "Is that outside England, sir?"

The old man smiles. Perhaps they do not possess maps in Ireland, he thinks. But then, he has never actually been to Toledo either. Claiming Spanish heritage is a required fiction. England's outdated laws will not suffer a Jew to live.

"We are Spanish," he replies, in perfectly good English. "My son and I came here, from Spain, about ten years ago. My family are bankers, and sought to open an office for business in London. The Mordecai Banking House is small, but well founded."

"I knew your son, sir," Barnaby announces. "I handled a property lease for him early last year. My condolences on his most untimely death."

"Yes, this terrible sweating sickness cares not for a man's race, or creed," Mordecai answers.

"How is business, sir?" Barnaby asks, and turns his sleeve, so that the old Jew can see the delicate embroidery. Cromwell's name is well thought of by the banking fraternity. He nods and strokes his long silver grey beard.

"It is improving, sir. We have your master to thank for that, I believe. He speaks well of us to Cardinal Wolsey, and then the cardinal speaks to the King."

Will and Barnaby exchange furtive glances. The letter is sealed, and so must their lips be. Instead, Will compliments Miriam on her exquisitely embroidered cloak. She blushes, and confesses that it is not her own work, but that of a Flemish woman. Will Draper finds her smile as exquisite as the cloak, and admires everything he sees. Hair, teeth, skin and eyes are, to his mind, perfection. He is a sensible fellow where women are concerned, and recognises the danger he is in from this girl.

"Have you business in the city today?" Barnaby Fowler is probing, seeking information that might interest Thomas Cromwell. He has seen the girl too, but she is just another girl in his eyes. His master will tell him when to look at girls, how to speak to them, and which ones to consider for marriage when the time comes.

"The Butchers Guild wish to build a new hall, to advertise their wealth," Mordecai says. "They must have two thousand four hundred pounds to do the job properly."

"They wish to borrow it from you?" Will Draper asks. He has a grasp of money matters, and doesn't understand why they cannot fund the building themselves. "Why, when they are already so wealthy?"

"They are a guild," Miriam explains, without seeking permission to speak from her grandfather. "A loose association of butchers, some of whom are wealthy, and some of whom are not. They cannot spread the cost evenly. So, they borrow from us, and each man pays back the same each month. This means that each man contributes evenly, and all can share in the esteem the new edifice brings."

"But at a cost," Will replies.

"There is a price for everything," the old Jew says. "I lend two thousand four hundred, and they return it, at four or perhaps five percent a year. Eventually, I will be helping to rebuild half of London. Perhaps the King might need my services, one day?"

"If the greedy Lombards do not return," Miriam says, and leaves the statement hanging in the air. Barnaby stores the remark away in his memory, whilst Will drinks in her beauty. The Jew is a very clever businessman. He borrows the money from investors, like Cromwell, and promises three percent return. Then he lends the gathered funds on at five percent. In this way, rich men can lend money without appearing to be usurers, and everyone makes a reasonable profit.

"The king will forgive them… but not this coming year," Barnaby says, softly, and the Jew nods his thanks. Such a morsel of information, from so reliable a source is valuable to him, and will help him gauge his future lending habits.

The boatman does his duty, and the craft makes steady headway, against the morning ebb tide, until they reach their destination. They exchange farewells, and part at the dockside. Will Draper watches the family, until they vanish into the tumult.

"A word of warning, my friend," Barnaby says. "The Jews were expelled from England two hundred and forty years ago, under pain of death, should they return."

"They are Spanish," Will says, and winks. Barnaby shrugs his shoulders in exasperation. How could the new man think of anything, other than his present duty? He plucks at his sleeve, drawing him out of the path of a lumbering brewers dray. Cromwell will not be pleased if his new young man is run over by a beer wagon.

The house at Austin Friars loses much of its glamour when Will is confronted by the greatness of York Place. Barnaby Fowler murmurs in his ear, explaining that there are several hundred rooms, and many miles of corridors to negotiate. The building was, until quite recently, the property of

Cardinal Wolsey, and is now the property of the king. Henry favours his new palace, and it rivals the great Palace of Westminster as the hub for royal court business.

"King Henry prefers it's grander state rooms, and much admires Wolsey's taste in wall hangings, furniture, and soft furnishings," Barnaby explains. "How envious he must have been of the cardinal."

There are guards at every door, but Will Draper and Barnaby Fowler are Thomas Cromwell's men, and passage is granted easily, often with a nod of recognition. Barnaby has been before, of course, and leads Will deep into the building's beating heart. Now and then, a courier, or some other household servant will stop and pass a few words with them.

They are Cromwell's creatures, and it does not do to ignore, or hinder them. The tittle-tattle runs ahead of them, and by the time they reach the outer rooms of Henry's Inner Court, it is known that they have an important message for the King. They are stopped, at last, by a group of finely dressed gentlemen, who swagger towards them, hands resting lightly on ornate sword hilts. Barnaby bows to them, a grand, sweeping acknowledgement of their elevated positions. Will Draper offers them a simple nod of the head.

"My Lord's, may I name Captain Will Draper, late of the King's army in Ireland." There is a sigh of disappointment from the group. The subject of Ireland is of little interest to them, as it is seldom more than a plea for more men, or more arms. "He comes with a message, from Lord Percy, the Earl of Northumberland."

"What? The whelp Percy writes directly to the King?" Thomas Howard, the Duke of Norfolk is a solid enough man, made to seem bigger by the broadness of his fur outer cape. He is first amongst the gentlemen present, placed just above Charles Brandon, the upstart Duke of Suffolk, and sails through life like a Man O'War, with cannon blazing in every direction. "Give it to me!"

He holds out his hand with casual disdain. Will shakes his head, and stands up to him. The communication is for the hand of King Henry, and none other. Harry Percy has said so. Norfolk growls and snaps his jaws like a bulldog.

"Bugger Percy, his father was ever the same."

Charles Brandon, the Duke of

Suffolk, who fancies himself cleverer than Norfolk, suppresses a smile, and beckons Barnaby Fowler closer to him.

"The King is with the Lady Anne in Esher," he tells him. Then slips into French, knowing Norfolk is weak in this tongue. "How do we resolve this impasse?"

"The letter must go to the Lord Chamberlain, until the King returns." Barnaby explains.

"That is too long," Brandon tells him. "My Lord Norfolk is a bully, and will start tearing out throats if he must wait."

"Then let the message be kept, its seal unbroken," Barnaby suggests, "and ask Captain Draper the right questions."

Suffolk smiles at this gentle hint. He sees the way forward, and sends for the Lord Chamberlain.

"Do you know the content of the letter, Captain?" says Suffolk.

Will Draper nods, ever so slightly.

"How is it with the cardinal?" the Duke of Suffolk asks. "Is he well?"

"To comment on that might compromise the contents of the letter," Will says. The Duke takes a purse from his belt and hands it to the soldier.

"We must await the return of Henry

then," he replies.

Will bows, and he and Barnaby back out, obsequiously. Suffolk hands the sealed note to the waiting servant, for safe keeping.

"Well?" Norfolk roars.

"The bastard is dead," Charles Brandon says. "The King will be devastated."

"I'll be damned if he is!" Norfolk grunts. Suffolk is younger, and less important that Norfolk, but feels the need to instruct the head of the Howard clan. Yes, the King, *will* be upset. Wolsey has been a friend and advisor for many years. Henry will mourn him like a lost relative, then look to see who whispered in his ear about so loyal a friend.

"Bugger!"

"Just so, My Lord Norfolk," Suffolk says. "He will recall your wicked spite, and the evil poison spread by agents of the Howard clan, and his mind will turn to revenge. Had Wolsey lived, Henry would have spared his life, but stripped him of all influence. That chance has gone now, and only base retribution remains."

"He will see how he needs *us* now," Norfolk says, convinced of his own great worth.

"How much does good West Country wool fetch these days, Norfolk?" Suffolk asks. "What do the Antwerp weavers charge for a bolt of cloth?"

"Surely, we have a man for that sort of thing," Norfolk replies.

"We do. His name is Thomas Wolsey," Suffolk says, calmly. "You have thrown the dice once too often, my friend. With Wolsey gone, who will hold England together for Henry?"

"Wolsey sat on his arse at Lambeth," the older duke says. "He was taking fifty thousand a year for his pains."

"And putting ten times as much in Henry's purse. Wake up to the truth of things, My Lord, or there will be all hell to pay."

"You seem untroubled, Brandon," Norfolk says, lashing out with the petulance reserved for powerful men. "Henry will remember how you often baited old Wolsey."

"In jest only," Charles Brandon replies. "I never wanted his head on a spike. By the time Henry has finished mourning, this country must be running as smoothly as silk through our fingers. If not, he will turn on you, and on your niece, if she does not produce a male heir."

"Turn on Anne? Rubbish. He would sooner cut off his own head!"

"Or yours, Norfolk. Or yours!"

"What of Wolsey's household?" Norfolk says, with sudden realisation. "There are men who know how to do things, and they can just as easily do them at our bidding."

"Make them your own," Suffolk advises, but tongue in cheek. The cost will be enormous, even for a duke. "I would start with the blacksmith's bastard."

"Cromwell?" Norfolk is not so sure. "Would he turn from his master so easily?"

"Wolsey is dead, you fool. Who else will he serve?"

"Well said," Norfolk agrees. He sees the way forward now, and can turn his mind to more interesting things. "How is that new girl of yours? I hope your poor wife does not find out, Brandon, or your brother-in-law, Henry, will be looking for your head on a spike."

Suffolk is blushing at the casual threat, and he curses himself for being rash enough to be found out so easily. Who is the fool now, Brandon, Norfolk thinks, with a cruel smile.

*

Will Draper opens the purse, and tips the contents into the palm of his hand. He counts swiftly. Fifty shillings. A good morning's work, he thinks, until Barnaby holds out his own hand. Being one of Thomas Cromwell's young men, evidently, has its drawbacks, as well as its advantages.

"One tenth goes to the master, and we split the rest around the breakfast table," Barnaby explains. In the long run, Will Draper will benefit. Some mornings, there might be as much as twenty or thirty pounds to share.

"Then I shall cherish my four shillings and sixpence," Will says with a shrug. "It will feed my horse for the month."

"Captain Draper? I thought it was you." Miriam is there, so close he can smell her fresh, soft skin. "Grandfather has business with someone inside, but the guards will not let us pass."

"Have you a summons?" Barnaby Fowler asks. Casual callers, even such pretty ones, are discouraged, he explains. May he see the paper? It is passed from the old Jew's hand to Miriam's, and then on to Will. Their fingers touch, as if by mere chance, and he is a happy man.

"Your appointment is with Sir James Fitzwilliam, but he has not attached his seal," Barnaby advises.

Will takes the paper from his friend. and demands to see the Captain of the Guard. He is told, politely, to shove off. He squares up to the thick headed Sergeant, and juts out his jaw. He explains that the pass is valid, and is told again, but more firmly this time, to push off. Soon, he will be fighting the entire royal guard, his friend thinks. Barnaby takes the paper, folds a sixpence into it, and asks the man to check the document once more. Perhaps he has misunderstood the order?

"My apologies, sir," the illiterate sergeant says, slipping the coin into his glove. Barnaby Fowler has saved the day for a second time, but Miriam smiles only at Captain Will Draper. They part once again, sharing long lingering looks. Religious differences fade to nothing once love comes hammering at your heart.

"You owe me sixpence," Barnaby Fowler says, scowling at his new comrade.

"Can we not share out my debt at the breakfast table?"

Barnaby laughs out loud. You cannot help but like this wild Irish Wolf Hound. Then he bids them hurry back to Austin Friars. There is great news for Thomas Cromwell to hear. There is? Will is at a loss. A message has been delivered, and a few shillings change hands. What is so important. he asks?

"Why, the Jew, of course." Isaac ben Mordecai, the mock Spaniard, is called to the Royal Court. Sir James Fitzwilliam is a distant cousin of the Tudors, and a trusted advisor to the Privy Purse. He arranges small private loans for the king.

Will sees then. Mordecai is important now, and Cromwell might want a messenger, ever at hand to visit him. The old man seems a pleasant enough fellow, and the girl… Miriam… is an angel. He ponders on the difficulty of her religion, but has none of his own to compare. If he pays court, she will disavow her faith, and join her 'Spanish' blood with his own… will she not?

"Get your head out of the clouds, Will," Barnaby advises. "We are at war, and there is no time for foolishness."

"War?" Will is confused. "When did this happen?"

"Why, two evenings past," his friend

tells him. "When Cardinal Wolsey drew his last breath. Master Cromwell must muster his agents, and shore up his barricades. For he will soon be at war with every idiot who wants to rule England."

"Henry rules."

"Of course, but who will rule Henry? Every landed lord in the country thinks they know how best to order a nation. We are, truly, a land of wittering fools."

Will considers this, all the way back to Austin Friars. He sees clearly that he might have joined the losing side, but it is of no matter to him. He likes Thomas Cromwell, and that is that. His mind turns to his next task, and he wonders why Richard Cromwell wanted it.

4   The King's Lady

The Welsh Cob is saddled and waiting in the courtyard at Austin Friars. Young Gregory Cromwell has tended the horse well, and holds her by the bridle. Will ruffles the boy's hair and offers a penny. It is turned down disdainfully by Cromwell's son. He is learning how to be a gentleman and, one day, all this will be his. He does not accept tips.

"She is a fine animal, Captain Will," Gregory says. "Has she a name?"

Will Draper shakes his head. It is a horse, won in battle, to suit his purpose. The boy is not content with this, and decides to call her Moll. She responds by nuzzling him.

"See? She likes the name, Master Draper." Gregory busies himself with tightening the girth a fraction more. Clever horses inhale when they are first saddled, he explains. Then Moll will exhale, and the girth loosens. An unwary rider can end up in a ditch that way.

Will thanks him, and asks if he knows how far it is to a town called Esher.

"Father says it is about eight or nine miles ride," Gregory replies. "He used to visit Esher Place often, when the Bishop of

Winchester was residing there."

Bishop of Winchester is a title held by the Bishop of York, who was Cardinal Wolsey, and Esher Place was his favourite home. It belongs to another now, and Will is deputed to visit the new owner.

"Here," Thomas Cromwell says, handing him a small box, wrapped in a piece of the finest satin, and tied with a yellow bow. "This is to go into the lady's own hand, Will. No others, not even the King's. If you are stopped at the door, bluster your way in. If they offer you violence, then offer it them back ten fold. Your heroic demeanour will appeal to the lady. Or so I hope."

"What if they kill me?" Will asks. He doubts that would be the case, but it does no harm to ask these things. One should know the rules of engagement, if nothing else.

"I shall be saved twelve pounds a year," Thomas Cromwell mutters. "Perhaps I should send Richard, or Rafe in your stead?"

"No, sir," Will replies. "I will do as you wish."

He takes the small parcel, and asks for directions. Cromwell speaks quickly, as if he needs to get the words out before he changes his mind. Will must ride fast, and arrive at Esher Place before the news of the

Cardinal's death does. There is a message, of course, but not one to be committed to paper.

"Go with God," Gregory says as Will digs his heels into his horses flanks.

"I fear Moll cannot carry two," he banters, and the child smiles at the irreverent response. He waves, but Will Draper is already dropping out of sight. It is December, and night will fall before four o'clock. He must push on, or sleep in a barn, or some haystack on the way.

Esher is in Surrey, which means a trip over the bridge. Will has never crossed the Thames before, and is eager to see the marvellous structure. He is disappointed. The bridge is clogged with carts, and women selling their wares. Will must dismount and lead Moll across, as much for his own sake, as hers.

A knot of men are standing idle at the southern end of the great bridge. They sum Will up, noting the sword, and the embroidered cuff. A Cromwell man, about his business, they realise, and melt away. To interfere with one of Cromwell's black suited crows can get a man killed with surprising ease these days.

Esher is a prosperous, though small town. In his day, Wolsey spent money like water, and the local trades people have done well out of his presence. They will be sorry to hear of his death, but will mourn it quietly. Esher Place is under different management now, and allegiances are like the royal pennants that flutter in the breeze, first this way, and then that.

"Who goes there?" The older of the two pike men at the gate has a stentorian voice, and his companion gives a start, as if he had been dozing at his post.

"A message for Her Ladyship," Will says, as instructed. Tell them a little, but in a firm, commanding way, Cromwell has told him. The guards look at one another, stupidly. After a moment, the older man signals to his comrade to step aside.

"Leave your mount for a groom, sir," he says. "You need the door at the far side of the quad. They will want your sword."

Let them want. Thomas Cromwell says it must be done quickly, before too many people become involved. It will not do for the good lady's confidants to be swarming around. The message is for her delicate ears alone.

He dismounts and runs up the steps, passing a guard, who has time only to salute. He recognises a military man, and assumes someone else will intercept him before long. Will is almost at the great chamber, as described to him by Cromwell, before two gentlemen step into his path.

"Ho! You there," the first man says. "Your business here?"

"To speak with your lady."

"Stand!" They sense something is amiss, and draw their swords together. Will's own blade comes out like a serpent, striking from its lair, and cold steel clashes. They are so surprised by his speed, that he is able to parry both blades, and step past them. The door is at his back now, and the two men are too shocked to respond. Will sheaths his sword, turns, and pushes into the room. A flurry of women scatter, leaving one, alone in the middle of the grand chamber. She is quite pretty, in a tiny, angular way, and is wearing a yellow gown. It is her favourite colour. Cromwell knows. The ribbon attests to this. Will goes down on one knee and removes his hat with a huge flourish. The men behind are still too stupefied to react. They should have cut him down by now. So far, so good. Cromwell may yet have to pay out his twelve pounds.

"My Lady Boleyn," Will says. "I have a surprise, and a message from my master." The woman appraises him. He is rugged of build, and most handsome. She is reminded of Harry Percy in his younger days, and gives him a tight, quizzical, smile.

"Who is that?" she asks.

"My master bids me tell you that the lion is dead." She stiffens at this, then waves the two gentlemen away. They have failed her, and will be made to do penance at some future date. She beckons him nearer to her, and he obeys. He rises, and approaches, until he is within touching distance. Will finds himself making a comparison between Lady Anne Boleyn and Miriam, the Jew's daughter, but it is like trying to compare ice with fire.

"Is this really true?" There is the faint lisp of a French accent, which creeps out, unbidden on occasion. She knows who is meant by reference to the lion. "Wolsey has fallen, so quickly?"

"Not to the headsman's block, my lady," Will Draper says. "He died, by God's good grace, peacefully in bed."

"His own?" She hates the man, and can't resist a final sneer. Will shrugs, and takes the parcel from his breast. Anne sees the beautiful yellow ribbon, and sighs. Will holds it out for her.

"My master instructs me to tell you this. He never had so good a master, and mourns for Cardinal Wolsey. That apart, he says that a good horse needs a good rider."

"You are from Cromwell?" She smirks. Cromwell is a spent force without Wolsey. He sends someone to plead for his life. "Is he too afraid to come himself?"

"He is busy, my lady. He says that if you ask, I am to tell you that there will *never* be an annulment."

"He dares to say that?" She is a shrewd woman, and suspects that there is more than an insult meant by this. She opens the parcel, and finds a huge, yellow Chalcedony Agate ring nestled inside.

"It is a fact," Will parrots. "There will be no more crawling to Rome, and you will be Queen of England within two years."

"Only if Katherine is dead." Anne would trade Wolsey's death for the queen's without a moment's hesitation.

"Not so." Will realises that his new master has predicted the conversation, almost word for word. Now, she will ask how it is to be managed.

"Then how will this come about, sir?" Will shrugs, and smiles.

"I am but the messenger, my lady."

he says. "Perhaps, if you summoned my master, he could explain?"

"Tell him to come," Anne decides. The gift is perfectly chosen, and the accompanying offer is very interesting. Besides, if it displeases her, she can always talk to Henry. Cromwell's head on a spike would be almost as satisfactory as Wolsey's.

Will stares at the proffered hand for a moment, encased in the finest of kid gloves, then realises he is meant to kiss it. He makes a hash of it, first forgetting to flourish, then actually allowing his lips to make contact. He is no courtier. Mary Boleyn, never far from her sister's side, comes out of a shadow and ushers Will outside. She is the opposite of her sister, all yellow hair and rose like complexion. Her dress is cut in the latest French fashion, and Will Draper is treated to an ample portion of well rounded bosom. She notices his glance, and smiles.

"Lady Anne will send word," she says. "Do try not to stab any of the nice gentlemen on your way out, Captain Draper!"

"Your servant, my lady," he says, unsure who she is. "Is she always that cold of demeanour?"

"You have come on a good day, sir,"

Mary says, laughing. "Most of the time, my sister is throwing things, and cursing like a five shilling Parisian whore."

Will has strayed from his remit. If you survive the giving of my message, Thomas Cromwell has told him, run for your life. He decides to bow and kiss Mary's hand. She lets him linger with his lips, then chases him out into the darkening night. It is a while since she has been in the company of such a man, and she wishes she were sending him to her chamber, rather than back to Tom Cromwell.

*

"That is a strange one," Anne says, once her sister returns.

"A most handsome one, certainly," Mary tells her. "He kissed my hand."

"Is that all?" Anne snipes. "What a novelty, sister."

"And what does Henry kiss?" Mary can afford to be insolent to her sister. She knows all her secrets, and it gives her a certain degree of security.

"Whatever I let him," Anne replies, and they both start to giggle, like little girls. She slips the new bauble onto her finger and displays it to her sister. It is the finest quality workmanship, and must have cost a pretty penny. "See, even the blacksmith's boy knows my taste. Where is George?"

"Our brother has gone off in a fury," Mary says. "The captain's skill with a sword made he and Edmund Conway look rather foolish."

"Then it's as well Cromwell's creature is back on the road," Lady Anne decides. "Else he might come to some harm."

"George is not that brave," Mary replies, knowingly. "Were he to call out Captain Draper... he would be dead in a moment."

"Then let him sulk for the nonce," Anne says. "Have two better men placed at my door... and have the captain of the guard flogged for his stupidity. What if the fellow was coming here to murder me?"

"I doubt two guards would suffice to save you, sister," Mary says with a wry smile. "Were it me he was after ... I would surrender myself to his mercy at once... and often!"

*

Will Draper retrieves his horse, and asks directions to the nearest inn. There is one in the town, he is told, with hot food and soft beds, for a man with enough silver in his purse. Cromwell's man thanks the gateman, and urges Moll into a gentle trot. It is quite dark by now, and he does not want another night ride, so soon after the last.

George Boleyn's feelings are hurt, and he will not rest until the upstart from Cromwell has been taught a sharp lesson. He is clever enough to know that he must not be involved, and details Edmund Conway to take four men and administer a beating to the fellow.

"For God's Sake, Edmund," he says, "do not kill him. Cromwell may be a wounded animal, but he is not yet dead, and might still have a bite or two left in him."

Edmund Conway has little stomach for the expedition, and delegates the task to a big bruiser; a sergeant at arms called Blackwell, who picks three more ruffians who will follow his orders for a shilling a piece. The sergeant charges Conway ten shillings, and Conway recovers twice as much again from George Boleyn.

Somewhere in all of this skulduggery, the level of chastisement has been mislaid, and four men, armed with daggers set off, intent on bloody murder.

When she hears, Lady Anne Boleyn will be furious. A dead messenger is no use to anyone!

*

"A shilling a night," the inn keeper says. "Sixpence for a hot meal, and another florin, if you want your bed warmed. You'll find either of my serving women ready to oblige. They are clean of the pox, and not that ugly."

"Just a bed," Will Draper tells him, and drops a silver shilling into the outstretched palm. "Is there a good fire?" The inn keeper nods towards a chair by the fire in the kitchen.

"Warm yourself there, sir. I'll have a girl take a pan of hot embers to your room. Drink?"

"Why not?" Will is not a heavy drinker, but a mug of decent beer will do no harm. It is then that the door bursts inwards, and a crowd of men rush in, shouting and brandishing knives. The inn keeper is wise enough to know when to slip away. Will is left alone with a quartet of men, with murder in their hearts.

"We come with a message from Sir George Boleyn," Blackwell sneers at Cromwell's man. "It is this, you worthless little shite…. *Know thy place!*"

*

"He really called you worthless?" Thomas Cromwell is almost shaking with laughter. "Rafe! Come here, quickly. Captain Will Draper is in need of your advice." He explains, with mock gravitas, what has occurred.

"Four of them, you say?" Rafe rubs thumb and forefinger in the point of his sparse, ginger beard. "I would have gone to the Inns of Court and taken out a distraint against them, forbidding them from any violence. Then issued a writ against the Boleyn fool."

"There speaks an honest lawyer's man," Thomas Cromwell wheezes, unable to contain his mirth. "Forebear, good sirs, Rafe would say, and let me issue you with legal papers!"

"There was not the time," Will tells his new comrade. "I was somewhat hard pressed you see… and their daggers were drawn."

"God's bollocks," Cromwell says, regaining his sense of propriety. "He cut them into pieces, and sent the whole lot back to Esher Place."

"Then we must consider a plea of

self defence," Rafe says. He does not see the funny side of multiple murders, and seeks only how to deflect the King's wrath.

"Not the ruffians," Cromwell tells his right hand man. "Their clothes. Will disarmed them, and made them go back, naked as Adam on his birthday."

"I cut up their clothing, so they might understand how cold a night it was." Will is pleased that his master is amused. On the way back to London, he had wondered if his actions might cause a row. To find himself, suddenly faced with unhappy odds called for swift action.

He recalls the speed with which he draws his sword, and scores its tip across an unwary wrist. The second man is more circumspect, but just as easily disarmed. The others drop their knives, and he sends them back to George Boleyn with a message of his own.

I *know* my place, he tells them.

"Imagine." Cromwell has not laughed so much since the last time he met with the cardinal. "Four bare arsed felons, hobbling back to Esher Place. I wager Boleyn was speechless with rage. Cromwell's men have drawn first blood, Rafe. Now we must write to Lady Anne and placate her. Tell her Will is a shambling, Irish bog born devil, an ill mannered dolt, and sends his humble apologies to her brother for besting him in so humiliating a fashion."

"Yes, sir."

"Then invite Thomas More to dinner tonight. Invite the French ambassador too. That should get things moving nicely. Who do we know who loves the Gospel, and can come at short notice?"

"Paulus Grynt is over from the Netherlands," Rafe advises. "He is known to have a kind word for Martin Luther, and hates idolatry."

"Invite him too. Seat him between the French ambassador, and More." Cromwell is enjoying himself. A less harmonious set of dinner guests would be hard to conjure up, but he has his reasons. The knives will be out, once news of Wolsey's death is abroad, and he wants them deflected from his back. "Serve up roast pork and pigeons with savoury sauces. They will argue all night, and hate each other for being so unyielding. If they fight one another, they might forget us, for a little while, at least."

"Shall we make arrangements?" Rafe

asks.

"To meet with Anne?" Cromwell considers how best to go about the delicate affair. It will not do to appear overly keen. "You say Mary Boleyn showed you some favour?"

"She gave me her hand." Will is sorry now that he mentioned it.

"Do you have a sweetheart, Will?"

"You should ask Barnaby about that," Rafe tattles. "Our friend likes the exotic when it comes to women."

"Stop teasing, Rafe," Cromwell tells him. "The captain is a fine figure of a man. Any young woman would swoon for him. Why not the Lady Mary Boleyn?"

"You always say we should keep our plans as simple as possible, sir," Rafe says. "Tangled love lives can become … unmanageable."

"They can." Cromwell makes his mind up. "Will, you shall be the go-between. If, and mark my words well… if… Mary wishes to pass the time with you, look on her kindly. Make a note of all she says, and bring it back to me. Understood?"

"Yes, Master Cromwell." Perhaps I might, he thinks. His natural instinct is to protect women, not betray them. Strange then, that he felt nothing but coldness towards Lady Anne. He is dismissed, and leaves Rafe and Cromwell to make their plans. As he descends the steep stairs, he hears a final word from Thomas Cromwell.

"Worthless, he said? Did Boleyn *really* think that?"

*

Moll has been watered, and brushed down. She stands now, waiting for the next job, as does her master. Will finds her an apple in one of the stalls, and feeds it to her, piecemeal. He considers the events of the previous night, and recalls how afraid he was when they came at him. Instinct will keep you alive in the heat of battle, and he is grateful that they were poor sorts, more used to robbing drunkards, and beating weaker men.

He makes a mental note to have his sword's blade honed by a blacksmith. It now bears a slight nick where it bit into the lead man's wrist. Perhaps he should have told Cromwell the full truth, but a half severed hand does not make for a truly mirthful story.

5   The Doll Maker

Will Draper is eating in Austin Friars large kitchen. He is not privy to much of the household business yet, and spends his enforced leisure sampling the cook's many and varied wares. He is just biting into a thick slice of game pie when the boy, Gregory, finds him.

"It isn't Christmas yet, Captain," he grins. "You should save yourself for the feasting."

"You keep the season well then?" He stands, and reaches for his sword, left hanging by the roaring fire. One of the house's many boys has oiled the scabbard until the worn leather is as good as new again.

"Better than the king does," Gregory replies. "An invitation to stay at Austin Friars is usually accepted."

"Usually?"

"With Cardinal Wolsey gone, my father's real friends are few, but he marks them all down in his books. One for friends, and a thicker one for his enemies."

"Then I must stay in his good book," Will says. The boy grins at the slight jest. It is no laughing matter to be in his father's bad book, for once written, it takes a lot to have your name scratched out. "Am I wanted then?"

"Yes, Captain Will. My father is in his study. He wants you to go forth and find him a doll maker."

Will is not surprised. In the few days he has been in Cromwell's service, he has learned not to be. Nothing is ever quite what it seems, and not one of Thomas Cromwell's men can say they truly understand the workings of his unusual mind.

"Ah, here is my dangerous wolf hound, my lord," Cromwell says as he steps into the study. The small, well dressed visitor is not introduced. He looks Draper up and down, as if appraising a horse, or greyhound.

"Is he up to the job?" Thomas Cromwell nods and smiles. He has since heard the full tale about Boleyn's men, and now knows the scope of Will's ability.

"Captain Draper is my falcon, sir. He flies from my wrist, circles, and swoops with unerring aim. I have but to name the prey."

The man seems satisfied, but still warns Cromwell of the price to be paid for failure. Fail, and the king will hear of it.

"And will he hear of it when we succeed?" Cromwell says, once the guest has left. "I think not, but we must do what we can."

"How can I serve you, sir?" Will thinks he is about to be charged with the commission of a murder.

"I need you to find a person for me," Cromwell says. "They are in London, and they make dolls."

"Dolls? Perhaps you should send one of the women down to the market in Putney. I hear anything is to be had there."

"These are not the sort of dolls one's children plays with." His master touches a small amulet at his throat. His own daughters are long dead, and he is reminded of it now. "We are talking about the black arts, Will. Do demons scare you?"

"An Irishman with a longbow frightens me more," he replies. "I think spells and ghosts are for old women to frighten children, sir. Are you troubled by a witch?"

"A maker of dolls. I am informed that this person is claiming to be expert in the making of graven images. They make a doll from wax, and in your likeness. Then you pray to the devil, and harm the doll."

"I have heard of such creatures," Will tells him. "In Ireland, every other woman claims to be a sorceress. The weak minded pay over their pennies to stop their neighbours cows giving milk, or for a love philtre to turn a young girl's head."

"You should have been born Italian," says Cromwell. "They believe in nothing, except the power of gold. It seems this particular doll maker is hawking a very special toy. For a fat purse of money, a doll will be fashioned in the shape of Lady Anne Boleyn."

"To what end?" Will is an unbeliever, so cannot understand why this matters. "Is Lady Anne afraid of this nonsense?"

"She believes in witchcraft, and that, I believe, is the key," Cromwell explains. "A certain lady might make it known that such a doll is being made, and that it will be used to destroy *la Boleyn*. If Anne hears of this, and believes it to be so, she may be harmed."

"Then let me seek out this doll maker, and dissuade them from their task."

"Oh, that it should be so simple." Cromwell does not deal with 'simple' things. The lady, it transpires, is a cousin of the king; then who is not? Every aristocrat in England is a cousin to either a Tudor, or a Plantagenet. Lady Hurstmantle's late husband's first wife was from Wales, which is almost like being of the blood to Henry.

"Duw yn achub ein heneidiau," Will mutters, and receives a raised eyebrow from Cromwell, who asks, in Welsh, if he learned that in Ireland too. He smiles sheepishly, and confesses to a Welsh sojourn in earlier times.

"Welsh and Latin," Cromwell says. "Can we hope for a touch of Hebrew soon? It might be useful."

"I have a few words of French," Will replies. "My Colonel fought with them for years, and often cursed me in the language."

Thomas Cromwell is a patient man, but time is money, so he gives a little cough to draw their attention back to the matter in hand.

"The lady in question is a staunch supporter of Queen Katherine, and believes Anne is a heretic who will destroy the monarchy. She harbours this doll maker somewhere, and the magician is known to be under her protection. She will spread her story far and wide, until Anne is in terror. Then she will let it be known that on a certain day, at a certain time, the doll will be used, and Anne Boleyn will begin to sicken."

"It is important to let your victim know," Rafe Sadler says, stepping from behind a carved wooden screen in the corner.

"I could hear you breathing," Will says. "You might want to practice holding your breath longer, Rafe. Ten minutes should do the trick."

Rafe smiles and gives a small, ironic bow. They spark off one another like stone flints striking, and enjoy the game.

"One must know one is cursed," he continues. "Else how can it work on your mind?"

"Do we know where the doll maker is hidden?" Will is not hopeful of a favourable reply. If they knew that, the witch would already be chained up in a cell.

"We rather thought the wolfhound might sniff her out."

"Where does this Lady Hurstmantle reside?"

"Near Shoreditch." Cromwell says. He has already lost interest in the matter, and is looking at some accounts on his desk. "Rafe will give you the details. Good day, gentlemen."

They go down stairs and visit the kitchen. There will, perhaps, be a cup of beer with a hot poker in it to scavenge. Someone is already there, being served with the standard bowl of hot broth and piece of twice baked bread. No one is ever turned away from Cromwell's kitchen, for he still recalls his own hungry youth. The man's head is bowed over the bowl, spooning the steaming broth into his mouth, but Will still recognises him.

"Harry?" Is it you, Harry Cork?" The young man jumps up at the sound of his name, and bows.

"Captain Draper! I am pleased to get so early an opportunity to thank you. Master Cromwell sent for me. I believe it is because you named me to him, in the matter of the cardinal's sad death."

"God bless his soul," Rafe says, without irony. "Then you two are friends?"

"I pray that Will thinks me so. When first we met, I drew my sword on him, and am lucky to still live!"

"A good friend then," Rafe says and laughs. "Have you seen my master yet?"

"No, sir. I hope to be taken on by him."

"Rest happy, Master Cork, he would not have sent for you as a jest," Rafe replies. "Knowledge of Wolsey's death was most helpful to my master. If he likes your manner, he will find you something to do, even if it be cleaning privies!"

"Even that is preferable to pandering

to the Duke of Northumberland," Cork says. "Harry Percy is a lout, sir, and he is not half of the man his father was."

Will pours out two tumblers of ale, and takes a poker from the fire. The drink steams, and they cross to a quiet corner. Rafe is, as ever, prepared. He gives directions to a Shoreditch house, and administers a few friendly warnings.

"Do not wear Cromwell livery. Secrecy is important. Do nothing to physically harm the lady. The king will be annoyed. Do not get caught," he says. "Else we might have to disown you publicly."

Will understands. Thomas Cromwell's position is very delicate at the moment. If successful, it is Lady Anne who will be pleased, rather than Henry.

Shoreditch is an odd mixture of fine houses and rows of filthy hovels, all jostling to find their own patch of sunshine. Lady Jane Hurstmantle's house is a new, timber framed mansion, with red brick walls. Will finds a welcoming tavern a few yards from her front gate, and settles down to watch.

He is about to order a room for the night, when the gates of Hurstmantle House open, and a coach rattles out. It turns left, and sets off towards Putney. It takes a few minutes to saddle Moll up again, but he is able to catch up with the slow moving vehicle in no time at all. The driver, Will sees, is armed. A short pike is propped beside him. A second man is sitting on the coach roof, holding a Genoese crossbow.

The Genoese bow is slow to re-arm, but is accurate, and can pick a man off a horse at two hundred paces with ease. Will allows Moll to slow to a walk, and keeps his distance. The coach continues on its way, and one hour later arrives at a remote farmhouse.

It is one of those fortified buildings most often found in lawless places like Wales, or the Scottish Borders. With enough warning, villagers can lock themselves inside, and defy an army. The style of building is falling out of use, now a well fired canon can be brought into play.

The coach stops, and a portly, well dressed lady climbs out. Even from afar, Will can see she was once a beautiful woman. The coachman leaps down and escorts the well dressed woman to the great oak door. He knocks, and they are admitted. Will dismounts from Moll, creeps forward, and waits. It is almost night when the door opens again, and Lady Hurstmantle comes out.

He is behind a bush, less than a dozen feet away, and can hear the conversation clearly. The woman is angry, and issuing dire threats against a skinny, long faced man, who nods and bobs at her every word.

"I will bring it to you tomorrow," he says. The accent is strange and his words are stilted. Will has not met many foreigners, so cannot hazard a guess as to his nationality.

"Do that," Lady Hurstmantle spits. "I will have the doll, or your head, *Mijnheer*!" The doll maker is a Flemish fellow. Will is somewhat taken aback. In the tales from his childhood, the black arts were always practiced by aged crones, with hooked noses, and besoms to fly on.

The coach leaves, and Will Draper considers what to do next. At last, driven by the biting cold, he moves forward, and knocks on the big door. There is silence, then the sound of footsteps. The door opens, and the thin man is standing there, holding up a candle.

"Lovely evening," Will says, and steps inside.

"You are from her?" the man asks,

his voice thick with Flemish vowels trying to crowd out the English ones.

"No. I am from another." Will sees that they are alone, and decides to bargain. "My master is not happy about your activities. He has sent me to advise you, *Mijnheer*. There are boats across the channel every day. Be on one, tomorrow, and you will live to an old age."

The man compresses his lips into a turned down smile. He has been threatened in every language in Europe, and knows how to deal with thugs who come in the night. He turns, and leads his visitor through a low door, into his work room. There is the stink of sulphur, and a dozen candles illuminate an array of bizarre looking objects on two long trestle tables.

"*U hoeft niet een heks lijden?*" He says. Suffer ye not a witch. How to explain to this stupid Englishman. "I am not a … sorcerer. I am a master alchemist. I study magical things beyond your poor ability to understand. You see this, yes?"

"No, I don't need to," Will replies. To listen is to take a chance that you might be tricked into belief. "I want only for you to be gone. My master wants it too, and *he* will not suffer *een heks*, my friend."

"I have a very good commission. Allow me to finish it, and I will pay you with gold from Lady Hurstmantle's fee. Ten English pounds for your purse." The Flemish alchemist is confident now. Money is the great healer, and ten pounds can keep a man living in the greatest comfort for six months or more. "She wants only for me to make a special doll, as a gift for a friend. See, here it is, waiting for its clothes."

"You mean it for Lady Anne Boleyn, I think." Will smiles at the cleverly modelled wax figure. Its face is as cold and uncharitable as the lady's. It stands no taller than the width of a man's spread fingers, and its hair is soft.

"Human hair," the doll maker confides. "It must look the part, or the lady will not want to touch it. Have we a deal?"

"How does it work?"

"Magic."

"Would you like me to cut your throat?" Will rests his hand on the hilt of his sword. The doll maker relents. Share the secret, make the fool a co-conspirator, and increase the bribe. In this way he will ensnare the stupid Englishman.

"It is to do with the painting of the doll," he confesses. "Twenty pounds?"

"I am beginning to grow very interested, *Mijnheer*" Will Draper says. Twenty pounds would buy him a modest house. How much is the doll maker being paid? And for what? A tiny mannikin that looks like Anne Boleyn. "What does the paint have to do with it?"

"Let me show you." The movement is almost deft enough to deceive the eye. The alchemist picks up a sharp modelling tool, dips it in a bowl of green fluid, and thrusts it into Wills chest. He steps back, and the point is confounded by the layers of clothes. The doll maker lunges a second time.

Will is ready now. He steps aside and grasps the man's wrist, forcing him to drop the weapon. Then he drags the man over to the table and demands to know what the green fluid is. The doll maker curses, but in his own tongue, and it is lost on Will. He picks up the bowl of green liquid, forces the man to his knees, and pours the contents into his protesting mouth.

*

"Poison?" Thomas Cromwell is seldom taken by surprise, but cannot hide his shocked expression.

"It was to be mixed into the paint," Will explains. "The doll maker was a man, a

Flemish alchemist. He was paid to make a life like doll of Lady Anne Boleyn. It was to be painted with a deadly poisonous paint. I think that Anne would cherish such a gift, and handle it."

"Good God!" Rafe Sadler is more used to account books, and is constantly astonished at man's depravity.

"The touch of the poison on her skin might have been enough to kill her," Will continues. "Whoever was to present the doll, must know the harm it would do."

"And who might that have been?" Cromwell asks. "Lady Hurstmantle is not a favourite of Lady Anne. She would suspect. It must be one who is close. Did you get a name, Master Draper?"

"I regret not." Will senses he has failed in part of his task. "The man tried to kill me, and in the ensuing struggle, he … swallowed the concentrated poison. It killed him within seconds, sir."

"It cannot be helped. A poisonous doll, by God. Whatever next." Cromwell shakes his head. He must make sure that Anne hears about her close brush with murder, and how his man stopped it. Then, of course, there is the matter of Lady Hurstmantle. The woman is dangerous, and vindictive. Having failed this time, she might try again.

"Rafe, a discreet note to Lady Hurstmantle, I think. Hint in it that we are on to her, and would frown at any further mischief from that quarter."

Will Draper discreetly bows himself out of the room. He has taken matters into his own hands, and sent a message to the lady already.

*

Lady Hurstmantle is an early riser. She climbs out of bed, leaving the young gallant sleeping. His labours during the previous night have been almost Herculean, and he is sapped of all energy. He has done his duty well, and will be sent about his business with a bag of coins. She regrets that she must hire her sexual pleasure these days, and curses her lack of a regular lover.

The lady throws back the heavy drape hanging across her window, and looks outside. She looks out over her well manicured gardens, and realises that there is something out of place, and that it is perching atop her fountain.

It is a full sized waxen head. She is intrigued by so strange a sight, and throws a fur mantle around herself. It is a frosty morning, and she puts on leather slippers too. As she gets closer, she realises that it bears a striking resemblance to her doll maker. How odd, she thinks. Then she perceives that which lies beneath a thin sheen of hardened wax, and screams.

The would be doll maker's head is a better deterrent than any sharply written note from Rafe Sadler. Lady Hurstmantle is horrified by the vision, and will take to her bed for the rest of the winter, and keep well away from the royal court. Queen Katherine will wait in vain for news of Anne Boleyn's mysterious death.

*

The news reaches Austin Friars at dinner. Thomas Cromwell's men, clustered around the long kitchen table, marvel at whoever has the audacity to do such a thing. To behead a felon, and then perch it atop a noble lady's fountain speaks of someone with a macabre sense of humour.

"I doubt it will dissuade her ladyship from pouncing on fresh young men in Westminster," Barnaby Fowler says. "It is seldom their heads she is after."

"Hush Barnaby, you know Master Cromwell dislikes too bawdy a house," Rafe says. He smiles across the table at Will

Draper. Should the truth ever come out, he is already formulating another plea of self defence for his interesting new comrade.

Harry Cork is notable by his absence. Will remarks on it, and Rafe signals with a raised finger that it is not to be spoken of. Later, out of earshot of the rest, he confesses his surprise that Harry Cork has been turned away, as not suitable.

"Master Cromwell was not to be turned on the matter," he says. "I tried, for your friend's sake, but failed. He sent him off with a few shillings in his purse, and a letter, recommending him to another."

"Another?"

"Anyone who might wish to employ a personable young man, I suppose."

"A pity." Will thinks of the favour he owes Harry, and regrets that he has let him down. "He might have made up into a useful sort of a fellow.

"Yes, it is a great pity." Rafe Sadler is embarrassed at how easily Will's recommendation has been spurned, so Will changes the subject to spare his blushes.

"Might I test your knowledge of London?" he asks his friend.

"Of course. What do you wish to know, my dear fellow?"

"The address of Master Isaac ben Mordecai."

For a moment Rafe looks surprised, then he bursts out into a gale of laughter. He fetches a quill and ink, and scratches out the name of a certain street in the nearby village of Stepney.

"I know you speak several languages, Will," Rafe Sadler says, as he hands the address over to his friend. "Now you wish to seek lessons in Spanish?"

"I wish only to pay my respects to the family," Will replies, but he has the good grace to blush at being twitted over his liking for the Mordecai girl.

"When love's arrow strikes, it is always within the bull," Rafe says. "It is madness, Will... but a fine madness, for all that. Good hunting."

6   The King's Counsellor

Austin Friars is in turmoil. Richard Cromwell is all for smuggling his uncle out of the country on one of the Flemish trading boats down at Tilbury. He and Rafe will stay behind and try to get out as much as possible. The king has summoned their master.

"Peace, Richard." Cromwell is trying to make his best coat look presentable. "I am called to York Place, not the Tower of London. His majesty would not play me false in this. It is not his way. Upset him, and it is an honest end on the scaffold, not a cat and mouse game. What say you about it, Will Draper?"

"I will come with you." Will is strapping his sword on, and looks every inch a military man. If it comes to it, Cromwell thinks, Will Draper will hack his way through a thousand enemy for him. He wonders at such ready devotion. He knows now about the waxen head, and suspects that Will refused a very large bribe.

Perhaps twelve pounds a year is not enough for such a man, he thinks. He must reconsider the worth of his devoted soldier of fortune.

"You will stay here," Thomas Cromwell says, firmly. "How can I offend the king by turning up with a murderous Irish wolf hound at my heels? Besides, I hear that you like to stroll in the well tended gardens of Stepney, each noon time."

"Then take Rafe with you, master." Will is genuinely concerned for his master's safety. "He can compose a piece of clever legislation to see you safe home at the drop of a hat."

"It is not needed. I have met with His Majesty on at least a score of previous occasions," Cromwell says, soothing their fears.

"Yes, but under Cardinal Wolsey's benign wing," Richard Cromwell tells him. "Now he asks for you personally, by name, Uncle Thomas. 'Send me this Thomas Cromwell' he says, and 'sharpen the axe's edge', no doubt."

"Then what do you propose, my boys?" Cromwell seldom loses his temper, but he is close to it now. "Shall we all run away, and live in an Antwerp counting house?"

Later, he recalls the stupefied looks on their faces, and smiles to himself. His ability to control them with his voice, or a sharp look, speaks of their devotion to him, and to his ultimate cause.

*

The King turns on him as soon as he reaches York Place. He almost scoops him up in his great bear arms, and drags him out into one of the cardinal's beautifully maintained gardens. It is winter time, and the bushes are mostly bare, save for some red berries, and a dusting of light, powdery snow. The king gestures for Cromwell to take the place by his side, and waves away the various lackeys who would crowd them in.

"You came, Cromwell," His Majesty says as they stroll along the path.

"You commanded," Tom Cromwell replies.

"They said you would not." Henry is flustered, and unable to draw his words together.

"They said I would disobey my king?" Cromwell permits himself to laugh. "Then *they* do not know me, sire. I love you as my master, Cardinal Wolsey did. How may I serve you?"

"I have need of a good, and clever man," Henry says. Rather than the simpering idiots about him now, Cromwell thinks. "I want you to become one of my counsellors, Master Cromwell. How say you, sir?"

"It is an honour, Your Majesty." Cromwell is relieved. It can often be the axe rather than the privilege these days. The season of the Winter King is upon them all, and one man's melancholic humour can change ordinary folks' lives forever.

"I need honest men about me. These are difficult times." Henry wants to talk in specifics, but cannot find the way. Cromwell, after all, is not even a gentleman. He has heard the tales of how he is the son of a blacksmith, who ran away to sea, and fought for the French, of all people.

"You have but to tell me your wishes." Thomas Cromwell is being disingenuous. He knows the king cannot simply ask. One must guess, assemble hints, and act. Then you wait, and hope you have read his mind correctly … or that he has not changed it in the meantime.

"I hear that your household at Austin Friars is growing in size each day." Small talk now. Tom Cromwell can be a patient man, when it is required. He considers whether the King can take the simple truth.

"Cardinal Wolsey surrounded himself with good fellows," he says. "I cannot see them starve, so I give them employ."

"Good fellows, you say?"

"And the best of their kind at whatever they do."

"Falconers? Farriers?" Henry runs out of *f's* and pauses for breath.

"The best."

"Send some to me."

"My lord Norfolk asks the same, sire."

"Does he indeed?" Henry laughs at this news. "God bugger old Uncle Norfolk. He has too much of England already. I will have Wolsey's own falconers for myself, sir. Pick out the very best of them, and have them put into my service, Thomas."

"At once, your Majesty." Cromwell cannot believe his luck. He will be able to put his people at every key post. The boy who lights the fires, and the man who saddles the King's mount will be his, and they will serve, and listen. "Might I suggest a fine fellow, who came to me from Harry Percy, just the other day?"

"I'll take him. Percy is another of those noble rogues who plague me."

Cromwell understands. The king is missing Cardinal Wolsey already, and seeks to surround himself with the next best thing. He shoots off a verbal arrow, and looks to see it land.

"This fine fellow left the Duke in disgust, I'm told, at the way he treated the late Cardinal Wolsey. It seems Harry Percy sought revenge over some petty affront. He refused him his lawful title, and withheld even the basic comforts from my old master. I wonder he stopped short of using leg irons, sire."

"I did not order that." Henry is distressed at these revelations. He owes much to Wolsey, and knows it well. "I was going to forgive him, Thomas. The arrest was but a chastisement. Do you believe me?"

"I do, sire. The last time we met, the cardinal did commend you to me as the finest, most loving of all monarchs. He confessed to having served you ill in the matter of your annulment, but said you would forgive him at the last. In his heart, he knew you would. It is only the acts of others that has stayed your hand."

Henry Tudor stands, arms akimbo, and a tear at the corner of one eye. He is as sentimental as Wolsey said. Then he takes Cromwell's hand in his bigger ones, and squeezes it.

"Lord Percy and the Howard clan have played me false, Thomas," he says. "I will take Wolsey's men under my wing, and you are the best of them. I am torn apart by my false marriage. How will I ever get free of Katherine now?" He does not expect a detailed answer, but Tom Cromwell has a plan for all weathers.

"The annulment will never happen," he tells the king, rather harshly. "The Spaniards and Pope Clement will not allow it. They think they have you in a locked cage, sire."

"Damn them!" Henry rages, but wonders if it is true. "Is that what they think then, Cromwell?"

"One cannot cage a lion so easily." Cromwell has found the right metaphor for the job. "England's lion can do more than roar… and his bite is fearsome. It will take two years, sire."

"Two years?"

"I could lie to you, then make my excuses in twelve months time," Cromwell tells him. "Though I know Your Majesty is a man of great intelligence, and can deal with the truth."

"Of course I can… I have a nose for

it… but why two years?"

"We cannot move forward until Pope Clement refuses you your annulment." The lawyer in him is in full flight now. "Once that happens, we can claim, quite rightly, that we were forced onto the path we must then take."

"Which is?" Henry asks.

"Ah, that will take careful planning… and the greatest courage on your part, Your Majesty."

"I have fought at the head of my army," Henry says. "Can anyone doubt my courage in the face of adversity?"

"They would be the biggest fools in all Christendom to do so," Thomas Cromwell replies. "Might I beg a few weeks grace to draw up my ideas?"

"Nothing disreputable, I trust?"

"I am a lawyer, your majesty. I live by my repute."

Henry laughs then, and can hardly stop.

"By God, but I have found the right man, have I not?" he says, at last. "They tell me you have the best spies in the whole of London, Master Cromwell. What then do you know of this business with Lady Hurstmantle?"

Cromwell shrugs. What should he know? The lady, he has heard, is ill disposed towards the Lady Anne Boleyn, and someone has done her a sharp disservice on that account. The King should rejoice at her discomfort.

"Perhaps the lady should stay home, and indulge her hobby, rather than meddle in a king's business."

"Well said, honest fellow." Henry slaps him on the back. "In my younger days, I was happy to be in that lady's saddle. I fear now that she is grown old and bitter."

"But still responds to the rider's touch, I hear." Has he gone too far? Henry frowns, then understands the joke. He roars again.

"Tell me the gossip, Thomas. You are the only man in England who has the courage." Cromwell bows, and begins a graphic account of Lady Hurstmantle's insatiable lust for younger men. The day wears on, and Henry spends the best part of it laughing at Tom Cromwell's risqué revelations.

*

"Bastard, ingratiating blacksmith's boy!" the furious Duke of Norfolk spits. From his high window, he can see, but not hear, what is going on below. Charles Brandon peers over his shoulder. As Duke of Suffolk, and Henry's boyhood friend, it should be he making the King laugh so readily, and the sight worries him somewhat.

"I warned you," he says to his fellow Earl. "I said to make Thomas Cromwell your man."

"He had already approached Anne."

"Then tell her to make him fast to the Howard cause. The man is here to stay… and already finds favour with Hal."

"A counsellor! A dirty common whelp employed as a king's counsellor!" Norfolk curses, and smashes his fist against the window frame in anger.

"If he pleases the King well, he will not be common for much longer," Charles Brandon says.

*

"Must he follow so close on our heels?" Will Draper says.

"Would you have me go unchaperoned?" Miriam replies. "My brother is looking out for my honour."

"Moshe, run along and play with your toys," he curses, but it is a good humoured demand. He does not want Miriam compromised. It is his intention to marry her, as soon as his mislaid fortune is restored.

"You would do much better courting me, Will Draper," Moshe replies. "I will not treat you as badly as my sister." He is just eighteen, a year younger than his sister, and is on the cusp of being a man. He carries a throwing knife concealed in each sleeve, and can draw and throw in the blink of an eye. Will has seen him pin a playing card at thirty paces, and admires such a skill. The two are already the firmest of friends.

"My grandfather is worried about our meetings," Miriam says.

"Where is he?"

"On his way to York Place. One of the King's men has need of him… or, at least, his gold."

"He must be careful," Will responds. "My master is with the King this morning."

"I think Master Cromwell treads a far more dangerous path than my grandfather does, Will." She reaches out and allows her fingers to brush the back of his hand. Moshe gives a theatrical cough, and they all laugh.

*

"How do you think we stand?" Henry is serious again, and is asking after the privy purse. Thomas Cromwell shrugs his shoulders at the question. What can he say? He is not a member of the privileged inner circle. How can he know what the nation is worth? "You must have some idea, sir?"

"I know that Cardinal Wolsey thought the country worth about a million pounds, and suspected it could be improved." The king looks at him, expectantly. "With careful management, I think we might get two million a year in revenue."

Henry whistles, and shakes his head in surprise. How? Such an enormous amount is almost unthinkable. Thomas Cromwell mentions the Kings most deadly rivals, quoting their wealth.

"The Spaniards have the New World, and the French are the most well managed country in Europe," he says. "We must take the best from both, and become a world power, sire."

"How?" Henry cannot see any further than his next round of arguments with Parliament. "Can we assume their ways so easily?"

"Policy, sire." Henry purses his lips. He wants it done, but lacks the stamina to do it himself. Thomas Cromwell's worth is becoming more and more apparent with every word. "May I explain?"

"In a nutshell, Thomas." Henry dislikes details, and has other things to occupy his time. "I must look at my stables this afternoon!"

"Of course, sire. We build a strong army. And ships. Then we sail the world, and establish new trade routes... or absorb existing ones where the competition is still weak."

"My war in France almost broke the bank," Henry mumbles. It is the nearest he has ever come to admitting failure. Fighting the French was a Pyrrhic victory, and left the king out of pocket.

"You do not use an army to make war," Thomas Cromwell tells him, as if instructing a small child. "Troops exist to give the appearance of power. Trade is the thing. We bring from one place, and sell into another, at a higher price. For this, we need ships. A navy. We go to the vast new found worlds, or scour the uncharted coasts of Africa. Where we land, we leave troops. They build fortresses. Soon, this is perceived as an empire."

"This is all very grand, Master Cromwell." He is losing interest, and wishes to be about his sport. "Send me details."

"Your new Lord Chancellor will explain it, and handle all of the details, your Majesty." Cromwell bows, and prepares to take his leave.

"You have promised me a new wife, and an empire, Master Cromwell," the King says, heartily. "I have chosen well. See to it, and you will sit at my right hand."

"Your Highness is too kind," Cromwell says, wanting to be off before Henry thinks to ask him the one question he wishes to avoid. It is not to be. Henry calls out, as he is almost free.

"Thomas, pray tell me … who *shall* I make Lord Chancellor?"

"Stephen Gardiner, at a pinch, or Tom Avery… they are both able enough men." Able enough, and quite manageable, he thinks, but not for the King's liking.

"Yes, quite. I though Sir Thomas More might do a reasonable job." Damn, and double damn. Cromwell does not need pious Tom More cluttering up the way ahead. Ask him to be reasonable, and he starts collecting faggots. He would as soon burn a heretic as pick his nose.

"A wise choice, sire," Cromwell concedes. "He is a man of strong principle.

Not to be deflected from that which he believes to be right."

"Hmm. We'll cross that bridge when we come to it," Henry says, with the utter conviction that he can sway any man to his way of thinking with his eloquence. "Sir Thomas More is a pragmatist at heart."

Sir Thomas More is nothing of the sort. He is a staunch supporter of Pope Clement and Rome, and will torture or kill any man back to what he calls 'the true faith', Cromwell thinks, but does not say. Henry is only seeking to balance things out. Every right must have a left, and every puritan his persecutor. If he can, Tom More will have Henry crawl to Rome on his knees, and kiss Pope Clement's papal ring, asking for forgiveness every yard of the way.

Despite knowing More is not the right choice, Cromwell will keep his peace. For even though they must come to oppose one another, the two men are, in fact, the closest of friends. He bows again, and backs away.

Then he is free. Henry has a horse to cosset, or a falcon to try out, and can spare no more time. As he finally leaves York Place, Richard Cromwell, Rafe Sadler, and four of his hardier young men step out of every corner. They are as well armed as a small Neapolitan army, and cluster around their master.

"What's this?" Cromwell says. Pleased at seeing them. "Would you have knocked down the palace walls?"

"And carried you safe to the Netherlands," Rafe says, in true earnest. Everything they have comes from Master Cromwell, and they would die for him, if need be. "How bad is the news, sir?"

"I am sorry to disappoint you," he says with a theatrical sigh, "but I have been appointed to the King's inner council."

"What? But that is the most marvellous news." Richard is ecstatic, and effects a little jig, which is ludicrous from so huge a fellow, and it makes his comrades smile.

"Yes, and all I have to do is get him a new wife, and an empire by the Christmas after next."

"A trifle." Rafe snaps his fingers, and laughs. "We shall start by conquering the Holy Land, and Scotland. Or would His Majesty prefer we invade France again?"

"Where is Captain Draper?" Cromwell asks.

"With his true love, I'm afraid."

Thomas Cromwell is disappointed, but cheers up when Richard discloses the sheer cunning of the new man.

"He tells me that he has been paying money to several of the guards at the Tower."

"His own money?"

"Who knows," Rafe Sadler replies. "His notion is that, if you are taken, it will be to the Tower. His bought men will turn a blind eye for him, and you shall walk out, a free man."

"The boy is too cunning for his own good," Cromwell says, but he is pleased, nevertheless. "Tell me about his girl."

"Isaac ben Mordecai's granddaughter."

"Ah, the *Spanish* lady. I really must see what can be done in that quarter."

"She is, alas, a Jewess, sir," Richard Cromwell says. He has no particular dislike for the race, but knows the law concerning their very presence in England. "Here under sufferance."

"Thank goodness she is not a Lombard," Thomas Cromwell tells him. "For the King is not best pleased with them. From what you told me the other day, our Jewish friend is being sounded out by the King's party."

"Of course," Rafe strikes his forehead, as though the light has just been let in. "King Henry is broke again. Lady Anne's courtship is a costly affair. He must turn to whomsoever has gold, and will lend it to a monarch who is out of favour in Rome."

"Correct." Thomas Cromwell is thinking fast. "If I could become the conduit between the King and the Jewish bankers, we might earn a small commission."

"And what of Will and his sweetheart?"

"The King might grant her and her family the right to call themselves English. Will could marry an English rose."

"If Henry does not pluck it first," Rafe says.

"The Lady Anne will not allow it," Cromwell says.

"The Lady Anne is being too chaste, master," Barnaby Fowler puts in. "It is reported that she denies him, night after night. Some think he might return to the sister again, if only for a little bodily comfort."

"Damn and bugger it." Cromwell imagines Henry bedding the sister Mary again. He has one bastard by her already.

"Warn Will not to become too friendly with Mary Boleyn after all. He might turn to her in the night, and find the King's hairy body in the way!"

The posse of Cromwell's young men surround him, and escort him back to Austin Friars, shouting, all the way:

"Make way. Make way for the King's Counsellor!" It is done in a seemingly joking manner, but soon, all London will know that Cromwell is the coming man, and must be respected as such. A word in the lawyer's ear is now as good as a word in Henry's.

*

They arrive home to find Will Draper waiting at the front entrance. He comes forward, eager for the news. After a moment, he recalls that a visitor has called, and tells Cromwell that a sour faced man is waiting to see him.

It is Sir Thomas More.

"What's this, come for a free dinner again, Thomas?" Cromwell asks, as soon as he enters the library. The visitor is admiring one of the books, but closes it, and slips it back into its niche.

"The king has sent for me,

Cromwell," More says. His face is grey with worry. "I wondered if you might have heard something? Have I grieved Henry in some way?"

Thomas Cromwell is about to make up a tale that will terrify More, but he remembers that the man has a family at home, worried as to why he has been called to York Place, and he relents from so cruel a jest.

"I have just come from the king," he says. "I am to join his council at once. We spoke about you, but in the strictest confidence."

"Yes?" More is all ears.

"He wanted my advice about who to make Lord Chancellor. He was for Stephen Gardiner, or even that dullard Tom Avery, but I advised he settle on a far sounder man than they," Cromwell says. He thinks you must seek to turn everything to your favour, and sees the chance putting More in his debt.

"You jest with me." More is wary. He sees lawyers tricks in everything Tom Cromwell says or does. He is not far wrong, of course.

"No. He will definitely offer you the post, my friend," Thomas Cromwell insists. "My advice, for what it's worth, is this: Do *not* accept."

"Are you mad?" Sir Thomas More is staggered at the ridiculous advice. "Refuse the King?"

"Better now, than later… when it will matter far more." Cromwell knows he will ignore the advice, and he regrets it.

"I will serve my King well," More says, haughtily, "and advise him to mend his fences with Pope Clement."

"Then you and I will certainly clash," Cromwell says, "and I will come off best. Think about it, Tom. Henry is the king, and he will have his way."

"We shall see." More says, standing up. Thomas Cromwell has done all he can to save his fellow lawyer from distress.

"Yes, I'm afraid we will."

"Stop trying to frighten me with your lawyer's tactics, Master Cromwell," Sir Thomas More tells him. "We have been friends for too long, and I know your ways too well. The King will bark and snap a little, then see the way ahead. Queen Katherine will return to court, and the Boleyn family will be packed off back to whatever backwater they swam out of."

"Old Boleyn's wife is a Howard," Cromwell says. "Norfolk will not allow his niece to be thrown aside... not when the entire future of the monarchy is at stake. Henry needs a son."

"If God decides he must be content with a daughter, then he must bow to His will."

"Then we must go to law, sir, and discover who it is who has the right to decide what God's Will is. A fat, lecherous old man in Rome, or the most noble Henry Tudor. Who do you think God would choose, Sir Thomas?"

"Blasphemy," More says. "I could draw up charges against you, Thomas Cromwell. Were we not friends, I would be putting pen to paper as we speak."

"Away with talk of friendship," Tom Cromwell replies. He does not know why, but he wants to save More from his own arrogance. "Put in your charges that I say the King of England must not bend the knee to Rome, and see how far it gets you. Now, let me have my men walk you home, old friend, for it is getting late."

"What...and have honest men see me in their company, and think I am of your mind?" Thomas More sneers. He sets off into the crowded streets. Cromwell gestures for one of his men to follow close behind, and see him safely home.

"There goes the wisest man in Europe," he says to no one in particular. "I would not want to fill his shoes from hence forth."

7 Understandings

Will Draper has never spent a more enjoyable Christmas time than under Thomas Cromwell's roof. The young men devise plays, and indulge in merry pranks, designed to surprise, rather than hurt. There are tubs of icy cold water balanced on door jambs, to catch the unwary, and flour parcels, dropped from upper floors. More than once Will has received a soaking, and a dusting with coarse brown flour.

He thinks hard as to how he can repay Rafe and the others, and comes up with a prank that leaves them speechless with admiration. He ties small sacks of ground charcoal to the heels of fighting cocks, and releases them into the long dormitory on Christmas night.

The household awakens to screams and roars of vengeance, as the birds bounce from wall to ceiling in a frenzy. Rafe Sadler emerges looking like a blackamoor, with a bird in each hand. There is a bad moment when they fear one of the creatures is free in the master's study, but it passes without mishap, and they end up drinking one another's good health until dawn creeps over the roof tops of London.

Thomas Cromwell indulges them, but insists they are all back at their duties without losing a beat. Business makes the world turn, and Cromwell business is now the King's business too. Between Christmas and New Year, a messenger comes, asking for Master Cromwell's attendance. The Lady Anne wishes to speak with him.

"Make yourself presentable," he says to Will Draper. *La Boleyn* is in town, looking over her new quarters in York Place. When the workmen finish, there will be connecting doors, from Anne's suite, to the King's master bedroom. Cromwell is informed of all this by one of the new staff, a boy of twelve, who passes throughout the court without being much noticed.

She makes them wait for an hour. It is her prerogative, Cromwell says. Soon she will be a queen. Lady Mary Boleyn ambles by, and pauses to pass a few pleasant words with Will.

"Good day, Captain Draper. Whom have you come to stab today?"

"I have yet to make up my mind, Lady Mary," he replies. Cromwell smiles and bows. The lady is certainly ripe for a stabbing of some sort. He wonders if Henry is tapping at her door yet. Time will tell.

"My sister will have adjoining rooms," she whispers to Will.

"A cosy arrangement," Cromwell says. His hearing is second to none. "I expect His Majesty is suited by the understanding?"

"I suspect not," Mary tells him, and goes on her way, giggling.

"Then it is true," Cromwell says to Will. "She still withholds her favours from the King. It might just work. He is a man who must satisfy his craving, and might promise… what … a crown?"

"How can that be," Will asks. He is learning his politics fast, and knows that two queens in the same realm are at least one too many for a conservative England. "Queen Katherine would have to…"

Cromwell nods, placing a finger to his lips. When he is called into Anne's presence, Will Draper stands to one side, trying to remain unnoticed. It does not work. George Boleyn is perched on a window sill, glaring at Cromwell as if he might thrust a dagger into his heart. The lawyer bows, deeply, to Anne, then nods towards George.

"Is the Viscount Rochford here in an official capacity, my lady?"

"You have a man with you."

"A man... yes." George Boleyn lurches to his feet, hand on the hilt of his sword. Will takes a casual pace forward, and Rochford retreats back to the safety of his window sill.

"Have a care." Anne is amused. "One day, brother George will be amongst the highest in the realm, Master Cromwell."

"Then he must learn not to be so easily goaded, my dear Lady Anne," Cromwell replies. He recalls when the Boleyn family were little more than farmers in Norfolk. Old Thomas Boleyn caught Uncle Norfolk's sister for a bride, and they are now of the blood. "Half of the court are still for Katherine, and would have Henry back in her frigid bed. It would please them greatly to have George killed in some stupid quarrel. My man could spit him in a second."

"Who would dare?" The Boleyn brother snaps.

"Anyone of a dozen men I know, for a handful of silver," Will Draper says. "My master is right. You should learn how to fight well before being so objectionable. I could give you lessons."

"Were you asked for an opinion?" George replies. Will smiles at him, measures him up, and gives him a mocking bow.

"The grown ups wish to speak now," Mary says. "You sent your man to bait me, Cromwell. Why?"

"My pardon, my lady. I sent my man to deliver a precious thousand pound ring to you as a gift. The words were not meant to annoy you. Did it fit?"

"The ring… yes. I am not sure about the words."

"May I speak plainly?"

"Can you do anything other?" Anne folds her hands in her lap and waits. Cromwell clears his throat.

"Pope Clement is under the thumb of Spain, and when he escapes them, it is to sell himself to France, or back to the Emperor Charles. Neither the Holy Roman Emperor, who is also king in Spain, nor the French king, want Henry to throw Queen Katherine off. It will upset their own church men, and give succour to the protestant clamour that is growing right across northern Europe."

"Cannot we buy the Pope?" George is unable to keep his nose out, and fancies himself as a first rate diplomat.

"Feel free, George." Cromwell subsides into silence.

"How much will it cost?"

"The whole kingdom would not be

enough," Anne says sharply to her brother. "Now be silent, or get out. Do go on, Cromwell."

"Your brother is right in one thing. We must raise a great fortune, as soon as possible. There are too many enemies to kill them all. Some will want gold, a title, or both. Then we must have good men about us; men who know the law, and can be diplomatic."

"You say 'we' like I have already decided to make you my man, Master Cromwell."

"I am the King's man, my lady." Cromwell makes the point as clearly as he can. "I want only what the King wants. He wants you as his wife, and that means we must ease Katherine from the throne. To do that, we must have men in Paris, and with the Spanish King, turning their minds away from war."

"Spain will not go to war." Anne has heard this from her father, who thinks himself to be knowledgeable in such matters.

"They will, if France does," Cromwell explains. "And France will attack, if Spain does. It is a fine balancing act, my lady. That is why it will take a year or two. Can you hold on that long?"

"I can." Anne smiles. Cromwell either knows, or suspects her methods. "Henry is sworn to me, and his honour is important to him. His one aim is to wed me, and make me Queen. Can you do it, Cromwell, or do you boast idly?"

"It can be done." Cromwell glances at George. "The king must be kept entertained during his every waking hour. We must arrange jousting, hunting, tennis, and … games. Surround him with jolly friends. With that done, I can put our plans into motion."

"We must look into the state of the annulment," Anne says. "It will clear the way."

"No, it will not." Cromwell flicks an imaginary speck of dust from one sleeve. "There is to be no annulment. The Pope will take another three years to investigate every aspect of the case… then declare the marriage to be valid in the eyes of the church. We must approach certain Cardinals, and offer them generous gifts. All we will ask in return, is that they hurry along the investigation. If they know we do not care which way the thing is decided, they will take out gold, and side with the Pope. The annulment will be dead and buried by next

Christmas."

"You confuse me," Anne says. The man is a master of trickery, and his words make no sense. "Henry and I *want* an annulment."

"No, my lady. You are confused indeed. The king wants only one thing. He wants to marry you. If the Queen dies, your immediate problem is solved, but I do not suggest anything underhanded. If she dies, people will say it is by poison, or that I had her strangled for you. Henry's reputation is all. If there is even a hint of scandal, he will not marry you."

"Then what do you suggest?" George Boleyn cannot hold his tongue any longer.

"Divorce, of course." Cromwell is surprised that Anne has not already considered the possibility. "Not a separation sanctioned by a corrupt Pope, but a legal document, approved, and sanctioned by the highest common authority in England. Parliament."

"Would they consent?"

"They best had," Cromwell says, "Or your uncle Norfolk will tear into them. Besides, the best part of them owe me money, or loyalty for favours past. Do you see the cleverness of it?"

"Explain… for George's sake," Anne replies.

"The King will be kept firmly apart from the process. He will have nothing to do with it. Parliament will enact laws that enable them to instruct the King in his duty."

"Instruct?"

"Yes. They will *tell* the King that his duty is to produce male heirs, and that he *must* bow to their desire. They will *force* him to divorce Katherine… much against his will. Then, there it is. He is a single man once more, free of all blame. He can marry your sister, without a blemish on his conscience."

"The church will never allow it!"

"The church? Oh, didn't I mention them before?" Cromwell rubs his chin. "I shall show Henry how corrupt they are. He will examine the documentary evidence from the commissions we will set up, and ask what can we do? Parliament will enact laws, putting the monasteries and abbeys under the King's rule. Henry will become head of the church, and the Roman church will be broken. A broken marriage, and a broken church. That is why I say it will take a couple of years, Lady Anne."

"With Henry as head of the English

church, we might see a more open approach to new ideas."

"Yes, My Lady, an English bible in every pulpit," Cromwell says. He knows Anne's thoughts in this. She favours Luther and his preaching over that of Rome.

"I will commend you to Henry at every opportunity," Anne says.

"Too kind, my lady." Cromwell is pleased with the interview, and will make a full written account of it later. His memory is prodigious. He is bowing himself from the room when George Boleyn's meagre brain splutters into action.

"You mentioned money," he says. "A fortune, you say?"

"Do not concern yourself about the trivia, my dear Earl Rochford," Cromwell replies. "Captain Draper and I are already in negotiation with a powerful overseas banking house."

"Your man does not strike me as much of a banker, Master Cromwell," Anne Boleyn says. "Can he even count upon his fingers?"

"Yes, my lady, he can." Cromwell is amused. "In Ireland, they say he had to learn his numbers, so he could count the dead men on his sword. One day, you will need him to count for you, my lady. I pray, and hope that you remember him."

*

They leave, and Will Draper is red faced with anger. Master Cromwell is taking liberties with his reputation, making out that he is a murderous monster, who has killed half of the men in Ireland.

"I apologise for my ridiculous exaggeration, Will," Tom Cromwell says. "It is just the one you have killed for me, is it?"

"Rafe says it is always self defence…. If I am in your service."

"Rafe is a good lawyer. He could prove you are the King of Lesser Bohemia, if he so wishes." He looks towards the end of the corridor. There are two guards at the outer court's doors. "Come, let's see if there are any great men paying court today." As they pass the guards, who nod to him in a friendly way, he cannot resist it. He cries out: "Make way, make way for the King of Bohemia!"

The outer court is occupied by a few of King Henry's older hangers on. Norfolk is dozing on a stool in one corner. Henry is off sweating in his enclosed tennis court, and servants are taking the time to rebuild fires, rearrange furniture and sweep out the old rushes. In the opposite corner to Norfolk, an old man is trying to make himself as invisible as possible.

"Pray introduce me, Captain Draper." Cromwell crosses to the old man and doffs his feathered hat. Will is uncomfortable. He realises now why he has been brought along.

"Sir, may I name my master, Thomas Cromwell to you. Master Cromwell, may I introduce you to Master Isaac ben Mordecai... a Spanish gentleman. He is a banker from...Toledo."

"Young Miriam's grandfather?" Cromwell shakes the man's hand, and looks as though he has found a long lost brother. "A fine young woman. My young friend speaks highly of her beauty, and of her amazing intelligence."

"Thank you, sir. I have heard of a Cromwell. A lawyer, they tell me. A man who can count the loose change in your purse, without need of it being opened. They say he recently took a great fall, along with a certain Cardinal Wolsey."

"You have been talking to Sir Thomas More, I fear," Cromwell says, sitting beside the banker. "My fall was but a stumble. I tripped, but fell into the arms of a great lady. A lady who will one day be above all others in England."

"Ah." Isaac ben Mordecai strokes his beard, cut in the Spanish fashion. "I hear cats have the same ability, Master Cromwell. Drop them from a height, and they land on their feet. Have you come to see King Henry?"

"I come to see you, sir," Cromwell replies. "Forgive my crude approach. Normally I would send a gift of wine or fine food… or perhaps a small jewel… to smooth my way, but this matter is urgent, I fear."

"You intrigue me." The elderly Jew could as easily have used the word 'frighten' instead. When powerful men seek out wealthy Jews, it seldom ends well for the Hebrew part of the bargain. "What can I do for you?"

"Nothing. It is the other way around." Cromwell glances across at Norfolk. He is snoring like a pig. "The King has use of you… no, don't deny it. Time is too short. I have a boy in your house who is in my employ. This will draw attention to you. Men will wonder what your business is with Henry, and some will resent you for it. Then they will look past your Spanish papers, and say 'ah, a *Jew* is amongst us.' Then they will wish you dead because of your faith."

"An occupational hazard, I fear." Isaac ben Mordecai shifts in his seat. "I deal with the King's man… not the King."

"It is all the same. I am having legal documents drawn up, as we speak. They will show that you were born in Coventry in the year 1465, and that your deceased father was a foot soldier in the pay of the fourth King Edward. You will be Isaac Morden, and your family will be named that also. The papers will be ratified by a great lord, and sealed."

"You have such power?"

"I have access to the Duke of Norfolk's office." Cromwell explains, softly. "One of his best clerks is a close cousin of my young man, Rafe Sadler. The papers will be dog eared, and aged with vinegar fumes. The seal will be utterly authentic, and indisputable in any English law court. Why, the duke can hardly condemn you as a Hebrew, when his own seal says otherwise."

"I still am waiting to hear the heavy price I must pay for such generosity." The old Jew cannot break his habit of distrust. He has heard of Thomas Cromwell from many sources, and fears what will be asked of him in return.

"I want young Moshe to join my

household." Cromwell tells him, and the old man smiles. A rose will be hidden amongst the thorns. "He will be trained in accountancy, and can act as a link between our two great houses. As for your dear, sweet Miriam… I can do nothing at all. For she will make up her own mind."

"That is true. I know she is close to Will Draper. He is a good man, but not a rich one."

"Captain Draper has a personal fortune of almost five hundred pounds," Cromwell says. "In addition, he is in my employ, and has many opportunities to better himself, financially. Does the girl have a dowry to bring with her?"

"She wears it about her person," the Jewish banker says. "Her mother left her with gold, jewels and pearls, to the value of about a thousand pounds."

Cromwell shrugs, as if to say, '*then why do we worry?*' and nods towards Norfolk. The old Duke overbalances on his stool, and crashes to the floor. He awakens violently, and starts to curse. Captain Will Draper bends, takes His Lordship's elbow, and helps him up onto his feet.

"God's teeth, do I know you?" He snarls at Will, half suspecting it is he who tipped his stool. "You smell like a soldier, by Jesus Christ's bloodied palms!"

"Captain Will Draper, at your service, my Lord Norfolk. We met here, just the other day. I had an important message for His Majesty."

"Yes. About that cur Wolsey's death, I believe. You are one of Cromwell's bastards, aren't you?"

"I am his man, sir… yes."

"Tell him to come to me. Tell him, I want him to work for me from hence forth. He can bring you along too, if he wants. I like a well set up man who knows how to wear a sword."

"Perhaps you might tell him yourself, my Lord?" Will steps to one side, and reveals Cromwell, with Isaac ben Mordecai, who are sitting, staring at him, their faces covered in smirks. Norfolk's face is flushed, not with embarrassment, but anger. He is a man of volatile temper, and finds it hard to understand why the old order is changing so rapidly.

"You are like sand beneath our feet, Cromwell," he barks across the chamber. "Shifting here, then shifting there… like… like… a woman's mind!"

"Any particular woman, my lord?"

Cromwell says.

"Don't try to fox me, you butcher's boy." Norfolk lurches up, hand on the hilt of his sword. Will wonders what the penalty is for disarming an Earl of the realm, these days? "You cosy up to my niece like the serpent twining around Eve's plump thigh. By Darkest Satan's unholy bollocks, you do."

"Ah, that lady." Thomas Cromwell smiles, benignly. "I am not the butcher's bastard, my lord. I am the blacksmith's misbegotten whelp, if you recall."

"What?" Norfolk knows he has said this at some time, but cannot recall when, or where. York Place's very walls seem to have sprung ears these days. "Why are you here anyway… you swine."

"Might I name Master Isaac Morden, my lord? A gentleman of Coventry. He is recently back from a long stay in Spain, where he was a noted banker."

"A banker, you say?" Norfolk conjures up a smile. To him, men of money are as necessary as whores, and should be cultivated in a like manner. "Call on me soon, Cromwell, and bring your fine new friend with you. I hate lawyers stinking guts, but one can never have enough bankers about the place." He stomps off, having quite forgotten why he was at court in the first place. Will Draper shakes his head, and smiles.

"You might well smile," Cromwell tells him. "Master Morden is quite agreeable to you courting his grand daughter."

"You honour me, sir." Will sweeps off his hat, and bows, as if the King were present. "I will make Miriam a good husband."

"Miriam likes fine furs, beautiful jewels, golden bracelets, and handsome men. In that order, young man. Do not disappoint her. Send one of your young men to me, Master Cromwell, and we will draw up a contract of marriage. Do you manage Will Draper's fortune?"

"It is lodged with the Galti family, who do business in Chester and Lincoln." Thomas Cromwell replies. "They are closely associated to the Frascabaldi banking house, in Florence. As am I. Will's yearly return will keep them comfortable, I assure you."

"Then I bid you farewell." The newly renamed Isaac Morden settles himself down. " I am to meet with Sir David Longchamps, to discuss a small loan."

"Sir David is by way of a sounding

shot," Cromwell tells the old Jew. "If you give the fellow favourable terms on a hundred pounds, his master, Charles Brandon, Duke of Suffolk will then seek terms for ten thousand. Satisfy him, and Henry will wish you to finance his kingdom."

"My people are not adverse to this," Isaac says. "Providing it is spent wisely, and is well guaranteed."

"Henry's jewels are worth over a million." Cromwell sighs. "The late Cardinal Wolsey left the King with York Place, Esher Court and Hampton Court, though much against his will. You might mortgage the three of them for another million and a half."

"Over two million?" the old Jew's eyebrows raise. "Enough to buy half of France. What will he do with so much, Master Cromwell?"

Cromwell shrugs. "Buy half of France, perhaps?"

"At least he will own better weather," Isaac replies. "What terms shall I offer Suffolk's man?"

"Five percent," Cromwell advises. "Then offer Suffolk four and a half on his ten thousand. That way the king will think he has a bargain at four percent. If you seek to raise capital from investors, I will put in fifty thousand… at three percent."

"Two and a half."

"Split the difference, and I will pay for Will's wedding feast."

"Done." They spit into their palms, and clasp hands.

"Have you heard?" The Duke of Suffolk appears from one of the long corridors, in a state of great excitement. "The King of Bohemia has arrived in court, and I am off to invite him to dinner."

"Good luck, My Lord," Cromwell tells him, "though I doubt he will have much of an appetite."

*

In the boat home, Thomas Cromwell reflects on the day, and marvels that so many happy understandings have been reached. He and Lady Anne have one that will replace an ageing Queen. Then there is the one between the house of Cromwell and Isaac Morden's banking cabal, and finally, between Will Draper and Miriam.

"A good day, Will," he says.

"If you say so, sir." The young soldier is in an ecstasy at the thought of his impending marriage. "I must tell Miriam that we are to be wed."

"Does that frighten you?" Cromwell asks, surprised.

"A little. She might refuse me."

"You should worry about greater things," he says. "Did you see how George Boleyn looked at you today? The moment he feels his place is secure, he will try to have you murdered."

"Does he hate me that much?" Will Draper is taken aback, but not too far. Men have wished him dead before now, of course, but none so highly placed.

"He hates you, because you have come from nothing, like him, but you have done it on merit. His advancement is through the King's love for his sister." Thomas Cromwell considers this for a moment, then laughs. "By the same reasoning, he must detest me also. Hey ho. Is not life both sweet, and difficult, Will?"

"An old priest once told me that it was like a great thorny bush. If you avoid the pricks, the berries are sweet."

"Did he tell you that in Latin?" Cromwell does not expect an answer. He suspects, as does Will himself, that the saintly man was more than just a good family friend. No matter. There have been popes and cardinals with wives and children beyond measure. Celibacy is not a natural state for a man, and it is a cruel thing for God to expect such devotion from his devoted followers.

He remembers his late wife and daughters then, and wonders if he will ever have time to marry again. And to whom? In ten years time, if he lives, he will be one of the richest men in England, and still be sleeping in an empty bed. Rafe and Richard expect him to re-marry, but his son, Gregory, is less sure.

It will take a remarkable woman to fulfil Thomas Cromwell's criteria. Perhaps he might bring over a sturdy Antwerp woman to look after him, or seek out a well read lady who understands the need for an English bible, and who can manage his many little quirks and foibles?

"The river is unceasing. It is flowing by so fast, master," Will says. Cromwell smiles, and wonders if the young man is suggesting it as a metaphor for the speed with which life is so quickly spent.

Thomas Cromwell is on the ebb tide. Ah, well. Perhaps he will content himself with watching his young men's children growing up, and leave the pretty women well enough alone. After all, he thinks, it is thoughts of such women in the king's head that might yet bring the establishment of England crashing down to its knees.

"Blink, and we are at the sea," he mutters.

"Sir, a question?"

"Ask."

"Where is Bohemia?

"I shall show you a map," Cromwell tells his man. "Though I doubt I shall ever send you hence."

"Then it must be further away than Ireland," Will guesses. "I hope he enjoys his dinner."

"Who?"

"Why, the King of Bohemia, sir," Will jests. "For he must be in court… as Thomas Cromwell says so."

"The lie hidden in truth," Cromwell murmurs. "Yes, it is a lesson learned."

8   Red of Hand

It is the end of January, 1531, and Austin Friars is preparing for its first wedding. Cromwell is as pleased as any man can be. The house has not been truly merry since before his wife, and his own precious girls died. When was that, he ponders? It seems more than a lifetime ago. He rubs a traitorous tear away from his cheek, and smiles at the young men busy tacking up bunting in every ground floor room, except his sacrosanct library cum study.

Lady Anne Boleyn is showing her benevolent side, no doubt in a bid to culture friendships. Henry's new woman has sent along a huge game pie, two cases of the finest French wine, and two dozen brace of game birds. Out of kindness for the young couple, she says in her note, but a seamstress, in Cromwell's secret service, at Esher Place tells an altogether different tale.

The Lady Anne never gives presents, unless it is to tie someone to her. Hers is a political form of giving. The reason for the gifts is plain, Cromwell's spy tells him. The news is brought to the house by a drunken brother. George is feeling sorry for himself, and curses the luck of a common servant; a man rumoured to be a priest's son, who is to wed one of the prettiest women in London... and fabulously rich with it.

"Pray, who do you speak of?" Anne asks.

"Why, the soldier, of course" George replies. "He is to wed the *Spanish* banker's grand daughter. God strike him dead!"

Anne is sitting at ease, with her women scattered at her feet. One of them leaps to her feet, and runs from the room. It is Mary, unable to hide her anger at the news. Lady Boleyn, begins to laugh. The seamstress says it is not a pleasant sound. She has never forgiven Mary for bedding Henry first, and finds her upset at losing Will Draper to be, quite simply, hilarious.

"Can she have imagined that Cromwell would ever let her near one of his young men?" she cries, and shakes with laughter. Mary has been paid out in fine style. No handsome young captain to warm her cold bed, for sure. "I must send a gift at once. George, my darling brother, what shall I give the happy couple?"

George Boleyn does not share the joke. If he had anything to do with it, the game pie would be laced with poison. Mary locks herself away, and does not reappear until Anne sends word that she is *commanded* to come. The humiliation is complete, gifts are sent, and the Boleyn household settles down once more.

The same seamstress tells of another Howard family visitor about this time. It is the Duke of Norfolk. Anne's uncle is spitting blood and damnation over being closed out of the King's latest scheme. Henry is disregarding his good advice, and fishing in dark and murky waters for a large loan.

"I have told him," Norfolk roars. "It is not proper that we upset the Lombard bankers. They are a link between Rome, and ourselves."

"And you, uncle?" Anne says, in her sweetest voice. "Are you not in debt to a Milanese house for fifty thousand?"

"Do not think to prick me, niece," Norfolk replies. "Your own father is indebted, and as for George… there is not a banker in Italy, or France, who does not hold his mark."

"The King will see his way clear to helping my family," Anne Boleyn says, and Norfolk leaps to his feet in a rage. This, the seamstress reports from her concealment.

"Your family?" He seethes and growls like a lion. "*My* family. *My* family, you ill got bitch! God's truth, but I damn the day the Boleyn's ever wheedled their way into it. I curse the night my sister opened her legs to your bastard father."

"Have a care, uncle, for I have the King's ear." Norfolk grabs her then, by the shoulder, and shakes.

"It is the rest you must be sure of!" he cries. "Tell your precious Henry to stop his scheming with Jews and blacksmith's boys. Have him take heed of his real advisors, before blood is spilled!"

Cromwell reads Rafe's carefully written report again, and shakes his head. The King is yet to confess to meeting with Isaac Morden, and thinks he is being clever. He plays Suffolk, Norfolk and himself against one another, to see who shall come out on top.

"And in and around our heels, the puppy More is snapping his jaws, like a good papal representative," he says. "Look to your immortal soul, and send Cromwell to the fiery pit. Eternity in Dante Alighieri's inferno is a better option than a visit from the Lord Chancellor."

"Master?" Rafe is only half listening. He pauses, and looks up from a list he is compiling. "Where am I to sit Sir Thomas?"

"Friends close, and enemies closer," he mutters. "Put him on the top table, at the bride's right hand. You cannot seat a man of his stature with lesser mortals."

"And you, master?"

"Down with the sweeps and poor pedlars," Cromwell says. "They are better company than any high born I have ever met."

"Will says he has no father."

"No." It is not biologically possible, of course, but he knows what Rafe means.

"But, master…"

"I say no. Captain Draper came to us less than two months ago, Rafe. You have been like a son for twelve years. I cannot act the part of his father at this wedding."

"Then he will ask the King," Rafe jokes. "For you and he are the two closest to him in all of London. Or, perhaps we might sit him beside Lady Mary Boleyn. She is a most comely woman, and I hear she is uncommonly fond of him."

"Do not let Miriam hear such loose talk," Thomas Cromwell says, "else she will box your ears for a month of Sundays."

"Then who will sit at top table with him, master?" Rafe persists.

"Me, I suppose," Thomas Cromwell

concedes. "Though I'd wish him a better father than I could ever be."

"He could not find one as good in the whole length of England, sir," Rafe replies, fervently.

"Then he should perhaps scour Ireland." Cromwell pauses. A small matter of business is niggling at him, and must be dealt with if he is to settle at all. "Did you ever find out about Wales for me, Rafe?"

"I asked Gwyllm Evans to investigate, when next there on any business." Rafe Sadler pauses, unsure how to continue. "He reported back to me, yesterday."

"And?"

"There is nothing to say. Will was a bounty man for a while, after Ireland." Rafe is uncomfortable, but no-one works for Cromwell without a full and proper vetting.

"Then it is more than one he has killed in his day," Cromwell says to himself. "The young man understands the workings of death better than he should."

"Have you seen the enormous game pie Anne Boleyn has sent?" Richard says, bursting in on them. He is a broad, hearty sort and, when he is not menacing people in courtrooms, or back entries, he is a man of immense good humour. A festivity seldom passes without him stripping to the waist, and offering to arm wrestle all comers. He wins easily, and never fails to boast about it to any who would listen.

"We must thank Lady Mary," Rafe says, chuckling.

"Do you think it is true?" Richard replies, nudging his friend. "If not, I would not mind warming Mary's bed myself."

"Careful what you wish for," Tom Cromwell says, sharply. "The queue for Mary's favours is long indeed. She has a gentle soul, and a most giving nature."

"Yes. She gives to the King, and half the court, I hear, and with nothing in return," Richard says. "A good lawyer would have drawn up a legal paper, before she loosened her bodice. I reckon such beauty should earn at least a minor house to call one's own."

Thomas Cromwell does not really approve of this rather smutty talk, but it is a wedding day, and such things are, by the general custom and way of it, allowed. Someone will, no doubt, compare Will's sword with another weapon, much used by new husbands, today. There will be much ribald laughter, and silly pranks played out on everyone. Richard Cromwell will want to arm wrestle the groom, drink far too much, and devour all the pies.

Such is life, Cromwell thinks.

*

Arrangements are going well when, at eleven in the morning, a horseman gallops into Austin Friars courtyard, at full tilt. The rider, a young squire from York Place, is shivering from the cold, and a glass of brandy is thrust into his hand. He will not release the hold he has on the sealed parchment in his left hand. It is for Master Thomas Cromwell's eyes alone.

Rafe sends for his master, who is in the process of having his new, fur lined cloak fitted. Cromwell is annoyed and holds his hand out for the message. The boy shakes his head. He begs Cromwell's pardon, but the message is written by the King… in his own hand… and must be opened in total isolation.

"The King called me to him," the boy says, still shocked, "and spoke to me in the corridor outside his private rooms. 'For Master Cromwell. To be read in private,' he tells me. Then, he says that I must die rather than fail in my charge."

"He has heard about your lewd designs on Lady Mary," Rafe whispers, digging Richard in his solid midriff. "And wishes to advise you of the best way to affect an entry!"

Thomas Cromwell goes to the study. He bids Will Draper, who is like a nervous cat on this special day, stand outside his door.

"See, boy," he says to the young messenger. "I am alone within, and my best soldier guards without. Rest easy. Go, and warm yourself by the kitchen fire. Rafe, see to the poor child, before he catches a chill."

The heavy door swings shut, and Will stands in front of it, feeling foolish. Is he guarding his master from Richard and Rafe? Or some unseen enemy who might come in, wearing a cloak of invisible wool?

Minutes pass. Then the door opens, and Thomas Cromwell emerges with the King's urgent message. He crosses to the fire in the great entrance hall, and puts the parchment into the flames. It twists, catches alight, and disintegrates into ash.

"We must go to Henry, at once," he says. Will has never seen his master look so angry. There is mischief abroad, for sure. He bows, slightly, then calls for a boy to fetch his warmest cloak.

"Rafe, can you tell Miriam…" he

turns to Cromwell.

"Tell her that I must steal her man away, on the King's business, and will return him in good time. And Rafe, tell her that I am profoundly sorry. If any guests arrive before my return, feed them, give them wine, and tell them nothing."

"You frighten me, sir," Rafe says, softly.

"I frighten myself," Cromwell replies. "Come Will. I shall explain whilst we are on the barge."

"Am I not to be married today then, master?"

"I am a lawyer," he says, "not a fortune teller. Ask me again before the day is out."

"What do I do if Sir Thomas More arrives. You know how the new Lord Chancellor likes to be early, and always wants all the news." Rafe dislikes uncertainty.

"Sit him down, and ask his views on Martin Luther," Cromwell says. "If that fails, feed him a generous slice of game pie. There is a better than even chance that George Boleyn has poisoned it!"

*

They are on the water inside of

twenty minutes, and the Privy Counsellor's sleek barge is sliding up stream, towards York Place, with a measured grace not matched by its occupants. Will Draper and Thomas Cromwell are wrapped in heavy furs, and sitting in the prow. Will knows when to keep silent instinctively, and waits for his master to speak. After a few minutes, Cromwell sighs, and gestures to the great, rolling expanse of London.

"A truly great city," he says to his young companion, "in a truly great country. Ruled over by a stable, honourable king. Henry Tudor is a man amongst men, and God's chosen instrument to oppose the black wickedness of Rome. Do you believe that, Will?"

"I do, sir. England has never been more at ease than under his rule." Will is worried at the question. Is Henry dead? Do Norfolk and Suffolk scrap over his body; each trying for the crown? "What is wrong, master?"

"The King has very great need of us, Will Draper," Cromwell says. "Something has happened. Something that might ruin the King's reputation abroad, and destroy England."

"Katherine is dead?"

"No, not Katherine." Cromwell is struggling to understand what has happened. "Someone is dead, and everything points to murder."

"Dear Christ. Who is dead?"

"Isaac, my friend. Miriam's grandfather is dead. Murdered, whilst alone with the King." There. It is said. Now, he will see the mettle of his man. Will takes a breath, holds it, then exhales slowly. Alone with the King, Cromwell says. What more damning thing could be known?

"And the King sent for you?"

"Yes."

"Then he is innocent of this crime, sir." Will mourns the death of his wife-to-be's grandfather, but cannot let it blind his common sense.

"You trust the King so much?" Cromwell asks.

"I trust no man, sir. Not even the King. If he has done murder, and on such a noble, venerable old man, he would wish to conceal the vile truth from the world."

"As would any man."

"Yes, sir. You do not conceal the truth by sending for Master Cromwell," Will says. "For Cromwell sees, and knows everything. The King is innocent, but fears no one will believe him. That is why he summons his best advisor. You are his only hope of a fair investigation, and his very reputation is at stake."

*

They are admitted to the inner court as soon as they arrive. One of the King's close young friends, Sir John Chappell, meets them.

"How is the King, Sir John?" Cromwell demands.

"Locked in his private rooms," the man replies, wringing his hands. "He will let no one in."

"We received a message." Will wants to know everything, at once. Sir John looks as though he will not answer, but Cromwell gestures for him to reply. Will is an extension of his master, and must be so treated.

"The King locked himself in, only opening his door enough to pass out a letter," Sir John says. "What should I do, Master Cromwell?"

"Be about your business. Keep everyone from under our feet, and, above all, keep your mouth shut." Cromwell raps on the King's door, and announces himself. The bolt is thrown back, and Henry opens up enough to let his new counsellor, and his man, inside.

"Dear Christ, Master Cromwell, but I did not know where else to turn in my hour of need," Henry says. Tom Cromwell makes soothing noises. The King has done the right thing, he explains. Now, he must tell all, so that Cromwell can arrange matters.

"Where to start?" Henry says, with tears of self pity welling up into his eyes.

"At the beginning," Cromwell says. "And leave nothing out, Your Majesty… lest it hinders our investigation."

The king is suffering from shock. He stumbles to a chair, and falls into it. After a moment, he clears his throat to speak.

"I arranged to meet the Jew here this morning," he starts.

"At what time was that, Your Majesty?" Will Draper asks, from his position by the closed door.

Henry is shaken, and looks to Cromwell for clarification. Why is this man questioning him without permission? Cromwell raises a calming hand.

"Captain Draper is my man in all things, sire. He has a way of problem solving that you will find much to your taste. Speak to him, as you would to me." Henry nods. If

Cromwell says so, then it is so.

"Nine o'clock. He arrived just short of the hour." Henry stands and leans against the fireplace's mantelpiece. There is a beautiful silver candle clock casing. The candle has been extinguished at some point. "I brought him in here, for privacy's sake."

"To discuss the great loan?" Cromwell is pleased to see the look of surprise on the King's face. In that moment, Henry realises that he has fooled no one, least of all his best advisor.

"You knew?" Henry is almost speechless with admiration at his counsellor's adroitness.

"I knew, sire." Thomas Cromwell does not explain. It is enough that he seems to know everything, for it will keep the king honest in future. "Will, what do you think?"

Will Draper is standing over the body of Isaac the Jew. The old man is sitting in a chair, his eyes staring off into the distance. There is a neat hole in his left breast, with a little blood around it.

"A single knife thrust," he says. "The entry wound is small, as if made by a very thin, pointed blade. Spanish, or Italian, perhaps. The *Dagoes* favour thin weapons. They are easy to conceal, and kill swiftly.

The lack of any blood is because the heart was pierced, and so stopped pumping. The chest will be full of blood, but that is all. I have seen such wounds as this one in battle."

"I had nothing to do with it," Henry says. "Nothing at all!"

"Of course not, sire," Will Draper responds. "Now we must prove it to the world. Isaac arrived just before nine, you say, and you started to discuss a loan?"

"Yes."

"Was he amenable?"

"We had common ground," Henry says. In fact, he was a fish out of water, and had little idea of how to negotiate a loan. Wolsey had always done such things in the past. "The amount was agreed."

"Four hundred thousand pounds."

"Yes!" The king is past being amazed. Cromwell is as shrewd and knowledgeable as his old master. "You are Wolsey's man indeed, Master Cromwell. The Jew spoke very well of you."

"I wager he did." Cromwell smiles. "What happened then?"

"I needed parchment, and my official seal. It was in the next room. I stepped out, for a moment, and when I came back, he was sitting there, quite dead. As God is my witness, Master Cromwell, there is sorcery here. There is but one door, and no windows. Yet not one living soul passed me, either going in, or coming out."

"A mystery indeed." Cromwell looks to Will Draper, who beckons him over to the body.

"See how he sits? The quiet look on his face?" The young man touches the wound. "The single drop of blood is beginning to dry. May I ask the King something?"

"If it will help." Cromwell has noted the circumstances, and is beginning to wonder what demon has been at work. "What about the chimney?"

"There would be soot across the floor," Will says. "Besides, how would the murderer know when to emerge from the chimney? Your Majesty, can you draw up a list of anyone who might have been in close proximity at the time of the crime?" The King nods. It will take his mind off the important fact that Cromwell already knows.

The death of Isaac ben Mordecai is a national disaster. If the King is thought to have murdered the man, every Jewish banking house will close its doors to England. Then the Lombards will return, naming their own interest rates, and Henry Tudor will be at their utter mercy.

"I will assist the King," Cromwell says. "The Jew's death would benefit the Lombards most of all, but do not let that be your main concern, my boy. I want the truth, no matter how bad it is."

Will Draper nods his understanding, and sets his mind to studying the small room in greater detail. It is twenty paces wide, and perhaps, fifteen deep. There are no windows. The walls are panelled with dark oak. The furniture is expensive, but sparse. There are a pair of chairs, one of which is by a small table, and the other in one corner, and occupied by a dead man, and a beautiful tapestry hangs on one wall.

Will crosses to the wall hanging, a scene depicting horsemen chasing a magnificent stag, and examines behind it. Oak panelling. There is no lurking felon there. He smiles, but knows he must look at this from all possible angles. Next, he draws his sword and steps into the fireplace. It is as wide as a man's reach, and tall enough to stand almost erect in. He pokes the blade up into the darkness. It meets no resistance. Apart from a little soot, the chimney is empty. Will crosses a murderous chimney sweep from his mental list of suspects.

He goes back to the seated corpse and wonders if he should lay it out flat on the floor. He has seen dead men before, and knows they will stiffen where they lie. If he is not careful, Isaac ben Mordecai will freeze in position, and they will not be able to get his body out through the door.

Miriam will be worried. Neither her grandfather, nor her prospective husband are at Austin Friars, and there is a wedding service, and a great feast, to be conducted. He should send word, but how? A written message will seem cruel, but a personal explanation, right now, is out of the question. Will has a job to do, and he cannot allow his emotions to control his actions. Isaac is dead, and the best way to do honour to him, is to find his murderer.

Behind, and slightly off to one side of the seated body, is a latticed screen, made of oak, but with inlaid flowers carved from sandalwood. It cordons off a small corner of the room, and conceals a pedestal, upon which is a delicate bowl, and a hand towel. The glazed bowl contains some water, with rose petals floating on it. Rose petals in January, Will thinks. The room is full of surprises.

There are fresh rushes on the floor and, apart from the candle clock, two lit lanterns. They are simple candles, their flames shielded by mantles made of the most delicate tortoiseshell imaginable.

"Were the lamps lit when you found the body, your majesty?"

Henry thinks. His hand is poised over the list he is drawing up with Cromwell. Then he shakes his head. They were out. The room was not well enough lit when he returned. He had lit the lamps, leaving only the candle clock out. Will rubs his chin with thumb and forefinger. Small ideas begin to come together in his mind.

The King has left a lit room, and returned to an unlit one. Will imagines him, fumbling to spark flint onto kindle. He lights first one candle, then a second. He turns to the clock candle, and only then sees the victim in the chair. All the candles were out.

"Do you know who did this?" The King is beginning to regain his regal bearing. He understands that his innocence must be displayed for all the world to see, but there is another, pressing matter. He must have a name, so that he can visit retribution upon them. The King's rooms have been compromised, and murder done. Henry must be seen to be the arbiter of justice. Only then will the Jewish bankers trust him again.

"I have an idea how it was managed, sire." Will crosses to the door, and tries the handle. It turns easily enough, but makes a loud grating sound. "What I do not know, is the name of the murderer. Your notes will help me out there."

"And in the meantime, I have a corpse in my private rooms."

"My people will come," Thomas Cromwell says. Richard and Barnaby will come, and transport the dead man, unseen, from the building. "Isaac ben Mordecai will be found in a lonely street. It will look as if he was waylaid, and murdered for his purse. Then I will take him to Austin Friars, and see the correct rites are observed."

"He was a practicing Jew, then" Henry says. "What do you know of these Christ killers, Thomas?"

"Captain Draper is to marry the dead man's young grand daughter, sire," Cromwell replies. "The family are from Coventry, but have Spanish blood in them. Your Majesty will recall that English law forbids anyone of Jewish origin to live in your realm. Therefore, this Jew was really an Englishman."

"You are a lawyer, sir." Henry tells him. "You use ink and paper to change a man's birthright. Still, I understand your motives. You must see that the girl is pensioned, Thomas. I dare say she will need it. I doubt you pay your young men that well."

"Captain Draper is a gentleman, sire. He has a fortune of his own, and a small estate in Cheshire. His family go back to before the Conqueror. I dare say his ancestors, some of whom are Welsh, are almost as ancient as the Tudors."

"Really?" Henry is amazed.

"Yes, sire. I read it on a piece of paper." Cromwell gathers up the sheets of information he and the King have been jotting down, and hands them to Will. "There, Captain. God grant you the wit to unravel this evil morning's work. Return to Austin Friars, and bid Rafe send Richard and Barnaby to me. Attend to Miriam, and set yourself to solving this crime, my friend. Catch this felon, whilst he is still red of hand!"

9   Too Many Suspects

Miriam is distraught, and is in her room, surrounded by the Cromwell women who, until now, were to be matrons of honour. Now they will have another role altogether. A terrible spectre has arrived at the feast, and sends a shiver of horror throughout the household.

Will Draper sticks to the story that Isaac is dead at the hands of a robber, and spirits himself away to Cromwell's study. He is just unfolding the sheets of Henry's recently penned evidence, when Moshe comes in with Rafe. Cromwell's principal secretary closes the door behind them and bids young Moshe take a chair.

"I'm sorry, Will, but Moshe is not convinced by your story," Rafe says. "He will not have it that his grandfather has been so careless. He also knows where the old man was going this morning."

Will does not have time to prevaricate. Besides, the young man is wise beyond his years, and deserves the truth. He tells it plain.

"Your grandfather is dead, murdered in York Place, and I must run down his killer. There are the bare bones of it." Moshe shakes his head.

"No, my brother. *We* must find this man. What can I do?"

"I am about to go over Henry's notes," Will says. "I am hoping to find a key to Isaac's murder within."

"And Henry?"

"Innocent." Will is certain. He does not want Moshe seeking vengeance on the King of England. "The King wanted your grandfather alive. He was arranging a large loan for the crown."

"Not so," Moshe replies. "He was worried because he was about to refuse the King."

"Are you sure?" Will is surprised. Henry seemed sure, but this casts doubt on him once more. "Henry seemed so sure."

"Our people in Paris wrote to us," Moshe says. "The great Lombard families are financing the Emperor's new war. He intends driving the infidel back to where they came from. They offered us a fifth part of the loan, providing we do not support Henry."

"That would infuriate the King," Rafe says, "but he did not know he was to be refused. Surely Isaac died before he could tell him?"

"Who knows." Will is suddenly suspicious. Rafe's face betrays a secret he does not wish to share. "Master Cromwell was doing a lot for your family, Moshe. Though I love him like a father, I must wonder what his motives were."

"Thomas Cromwell is a fine man."

"I agree," Will Draper says, "but even an honest man must turn a profit. What say you, Rafe?"

"This is not any of your business, Will," Rafe says.

"No, murder is my current business," says Will. "Must I return to York Place, and ask Master Cromwell the truth of things, in front of Henry?"

"For God's sake, no!" Rafe is upset, and wishes his master were here to answer. "Our master did it for us all. He did it so Miriam was not a heathen Christ killer any more, and you could wed her. He did it because he wanted to train Moshe in the art of law. And he did it, because he could not help himself. Master Cromwell is a consummate man of business."

"Tell me." Will is almost there. Cromwell can never turn away from a good deal, and sought out Isaac for a reason. Moshe spills out the truth, to save Rafe's blushes.

"Your master came to an arrangement with the Mordecai bank," he says. "We were to refuse the loan this morning. Then Henry would be at his wits end. Where to go? Ah, but I shall ask my dear friend, Cromwell what to do! Master Cromwell has already arranged to borrow the bulk of the money from us, using himself as guarantee. He will sooth your King, offering to lend to him at five percent. We will charge four percent. Henry is overjoyed with Cromwell, and Cromwell is four thousand pounds a year richer."

"I see. Then I can cross both he, and Henry, off my list of suspects," Will says. "Thomas Cromwell, like the king, needed poor Isaac very much alive."

"No one would wish my grandfather dead," Moshe tells them. "A kinder soul never existed. It makes no sense."

Will agrees. Isaac ben Mordecai is known for his benevolence towards the poor, his generosity to the homeless, and his fair minded way with those looking to borrow from him. Had he been a Christian, the man might have qualified to become a saint.

Nevertheless, Will Draper thinks, the man still lies murdered, and mourned downstairs.

*

Will begins to read King Henry's recollections of the morning. He remembers a boy bringing in a bowl of fresh water, and another sweeping out the old rushes. Both jobs would normally have been done long before Henry wakes, but this morning is different. He has an early visitor and is up and dressed by eight. Outside his door, Sir John Chappell loiters, in case he is needed, and in the outer chamber Charles Brandon, Earl of Suffolk has arrived early, accompanied by the gristly Norfolk.

The king's memory is good, and he recalls seeing Sir Edward Francis chatting with Master Jolly, the dance master, George Boleyn, and Sir Edmund Prosser, an old bowls companion. Then there are the young men who inhabit every court. Cromwell has his, and Henry is not deficient. There is the musician fellow, who Lady Anne likes, and whose name he does not know, and a useful young chap, recently recommended by Thomas Cromwell.

Here, in brackets, Cromwell has scratched the name *(Harry Cork)*. Young Harry from Leicester, who first pointed him at Master Cromwell and helped further his career. Will smiles at this. Cromwell places people everywhere. He has eyes and ears throughout the realm. Then Henry names Harry Percy, Duke of Northumberland, in court with his lieutenant, the redoubtable Sir Andrew Jennings.

Henry's courtiers are, on the whole, not early risers, so the list is fairly short. Thomas Cromwell's hand has written, hurriedly, the last half page. He says:

> *There are sundry guards and servants, whose names are unknown. A word with the Master of the Halls will reveal who they are. I must suggest another name. One which Henry has not recalled. My information leads me to believe that Lady Mary Boleyn might have been about. Her presence close to the King is sensitive. Have a care.*

Will curses under his breath. Lady Anne plays the virgin, and her sister Mary plays the whore. Henry is keeping it in the family. The Duke of Norfolk's nieces are doing his clan proud. If Mary was with Henry, the king would never admit it, for fear of Anne Boleyn finding out.

"Did Isaac know the Duke of Norfolk?" Will asks. Moshe is not comfortable with such direct questions. He has been taught to preserve his family's secrets.

"They had business," he confesses. "Norfolk wants to live like a great lord, but has not the gold. Grandfather arranged a loan of ten thousand, using his holdings in East Anglia as security. He was late with his payments."

"What about Charles Brandon?"

"Suffolk?" Moshe almost chokes laughing. "We lent him two thousand, against several sheep farms near Ipswich. He gambled it away at cards, and defaulted. The farms were already mortgaged with a local wool merchant, and Brandon had forgotten to mention it to us. Master Cromwell is handling the legal work for us, and hopes to recoup the loan without too much disgrace for His Lordship. As you know, Jews have no legal rights, and can be cheated with impunity. Becoming English citizens means we can now chase defaulters through the law courts, until they must pay."

"So, Suffolk would be unhappy with Isaac's new status?" Will has his first real suspect. What might a desperate man do to save two thousand pounds? It was enough to buy the whole of Southwark, with change left over. But would the man, a respected noble, actually soil his own hands?

"You think Suffolk did it?" Moshe asks.

"Let us not run before learning to walk, Master Moshe," Will tells him. "What else do we know about Charles Brandon, Rafe?"

"He owes money to the Lombard bankers too. His marriage to the king's youngest sister is all that keeps the wolves at bay," Rafe says. "He is a poor gambler, and an insatiable womaniser. It is rumoured that he keeps a young mistress, well away from court. Should henry find out, their friendship would be battered, and might even end."

"Is he the sort who could kill?" Will asks.

"Three years ago, a man over in Norwich accused him of bribing a tax collector. Suffolk wanted his neighbours sheep pasture, so had the tax gatherer recalculate the farmer's indebtedness. It was clumsily done, and the man, quite rightly, complained to the county's sheriff. Before it went to law, the man was waylaid in the street, and brutally stabbed to death. Suffolk was drinking in a nearby inn when it happened, surrounded by a dozen helpful witnesses. The killers were never found, and Suffolk's innocence was never queried."

"This morning, he made sure he was with Norfolk," Will Draper says. "He sticks to the man, like shit to a sheep's fleece."

"The Duke of Norfolk is old blood," Rafe explains. "Brandon was nothing, until he married Henry's sister, without his blessing. The King would have taken his head, save for their childhood friendship. Even so, he had to leave the court, and hide away in Suffolk for twelve months. He uses Norfolk now as a sort of a shield."

"Would Norfolk kill to avoid paying a debt?"

"Why?" Moshe asks. "He is the greatest man in England, save for Henry. He can raise ten thousand armed men within a month, and keeps Henry's peace for him. Then there is his niece. Once she marries King Henry, the Duke of Norfolk will be the King's closest blood."

"What if Henry tires of Lady Anne?" Will asks. Moshe shrugs, but Rafe grins. He blows an airy kiss into the room.

"The King cannot leave an unknown

fruit uneaten. He is curious, like most men, as to what a woman is like. Lady Anne is the forbidden fruit. Henry will move the heavens themselves to have her in his bed, but so far, his endeavours have foundered. She will not consent to sexual congress with the king, until the ring is placed on her finger."

"And what about Lady Mary?" Will thinks it unlikely that a woman would kill with a knife, but stranger things have happened.

"Rumour has it," Rafe says, "that her child is Henry's bastard, and that she still holds his interest. She is a most desirable woman, and she knows it."

"Be careful not to misconstrue things," Moshe says. He is new to Austin Friars, but already his devotion to facts, and evidence is firmly in place. "The King might just be being kind to the lady, because of their past liaison."

Rafe and Will exchange smiles. It is easy to be kind to a beautiful woman. She must be spoken to. Will makes a note. It is for him to do, as soon as possible, and without upsetting the King.

"Do we know why Lord Percy is at court?" Will asks his comrades. Rafe Sadler raises an eyebrow at this news. Harry Percy is the guardian of the northern border with the Scots, and should not be in the south at all. To leave the Scots unwatched is like kicking a nest of angry wasps, and hoping not to be stung. It amounts to dereliction of duty, and cannot be readily explained away.

"You must ask him, I suppose," Rafe tells his friend. "The King is still angry with the Duke of Northumberland over Cardinal Wolsey's death. He blames him for being far too heavy handed over the poor old fellow's arrest."

"How do you arrest someone in a light handed way?" Will Draper wants to know.

"The King misses Wolsey," Moshe puts in. "It is why he loves Cromwell so much. He thinks our master is a sorcerer too."

"That is quite enough of that talk," Will Draper tells the young man. "The king is already half convinced that black arts are involved in your grandfather's murder. He thinks an evil spirit slipped under the door with a dagger in its teeth."

"How long was Henry out of the room?"

"I thought of that, Rafe. He has a suite of rooms along the west corridor. Two adjoining rooms on one side, and two more directly across the way, Henry closed the door behind him, for privacy's sake, and crossed to the opposite room. His seal of office was in a cabinet there, you see. He left this second door ajar, and could see the door to where Isaac was waiting. No one came near it, or so he swears. He retrieved the seal, some ink and a roll of parchment, and went back into the first room."

"To find my grandfather dead." Moshe made a sucking noise with his teeth. "If Henry was not your king, the hangman's noose would already be about his neck, Master Will."

"I cannot rush matters," Will replies. "The innocent must have their say, if we are to trap the guilty."

"Besides, the king has nothing to gain with Isaac's death," Rafe says, again. They go around in circles for a little while longer, then Will Draper decides to return to York Place. There are difficult questions waiting to be asked, and he cannot put things off any longer. Each hour that passes makes it more difficult to bring the culprit to justice, Will thinks, and then he wonders how things will go if he finds the murderer to be someone close to the throne.

True, a lady would probably not use a knife, but she might well drop a bag of gold into the hand of an available assassin. Then again, how desperate are the great lords of England to escape their debts? Has Suffolk the nerve to act, or Norfolk the ability, to carry out so cold blooded a murder?

*

"Here, take this." Thomas Cromwell hands Will Draper a folded parchment. It has Henry's own wax seal on it. "A hand written warrant from the King is a rare thing, my boy. It commands any, and all, of his subjects to put themselves at your complete disposal. You may ask what soever you like, of whomsoever ever you like."

"Anyone?" Will wonders if either Norfolk or Suffolk would obey such a document, and smiles to himself. He must put it to the test, soon, and see what happens.

"The King understands that you will be most discreet over the matter of Lady Mary Boleyn's presence last night." Thomas Cromwell understands the importance of discretion. There are things locked away in his memory that no man should know, and live. "She is waiting in the next room to where the murder was done. I suggest you speak to her now, before anything else. Then I suggest that you get her in a coach, and back to Esher, before Lady Anne begins to sniff around. Her presence at court was not authorised, you see. It will not do to have anyone suspect."

"To suspect what, Master Thomas?" Will Draper asks, his face as open as a choirboy's. Cromwell cannot help but grin at his reaction. Will Draper will go far in his employ.

"She is unchaperoned," he says, with a sly wink. "Keep the table between you at all times, Will!"

"I do not believe the lady is as you think, sir," Will says. "I hear only of the king drinking from her cup. The girl might wish for a younger lover, but I doubt she has ever been unfaithful to the king."

"Perhaps not," Cromwell concedes. "She is not a stupid girl, and must know the king would frown on anyone else paying her attention. Her devotion to the king cannot be denied... and her bastard child attests to that."

"Then he is the father?"Will asks, and Thomas Cromwell nods his answer, whilst placing a finger to his lips.

"Let us stick to the facts, Will," he

advises, "and leave the gossip to the ladies of the court. They have time to idle away in silliness, whereas we do not."

"Then wish me luck," Will says, "and rescue me, if I call for help!"

*

Lady Mary Boleyn is utterly bored. She expects Henry to arrive at any moment, with a suitable thank you gift for the night before when, once more, she had to put up with his infantile groping. Instead, the door opens, and Captain Draper slides in to her presence. Her face betrays surprise, and then she smiles, a glowing smile that would gladden any man's heart.

"My lady." He bows.

"Have you come from the King?" she asks.

"I have, Lady Mary." Will holds out his warrant. "He commands me to ask you questions about the tragic events of this morning."

"Has he then lost his tongue?" Mary Boleyn says, hurt that the king thinks a messenger will suffice... even such an attractive one. "He put it to a fine enough use last night." The picture this remark conjures up is not edifying to Will Draper, and he pushes it, firmly, to one side.

"What time did His Majesty leave you this morning?"

"They teach impertinence in Ireland these days, do they?" Lady Mary snaps at him.

"Forgive me, but I must have answers." He opens the letter from Henry, and urges her to read it. She cannot hide her surprise. The King has given Captain Draper a powerful weapon, and she can no longer play the part of the affronted virgin, without going against the king's explicitly written down wishes.

"He rose about seven, and left my chamber. I dressed, and followed about eight thirty."

"Are you sure of the time?"

The odd half hour was of little importance around the court, with only a few rooms furnished with candle clocks or hourglasses, but Henry's suite is furnished better than any other part of the palace, thanks to Wolsey.

"The clock in this room was lit up. It showed the time well enough."

"It was lit?" Will is confused, but cannot put his finger on that which causes it.

"Of course. What is this all about, Will?" She moves closer, and the young man sidles away, keeping a respectable distance between them both.

"Did you hear any noises from next door?"

"The King's office?" She frowns. "Not that I recall. I was in here until just shy of nine, then left to walk in the garden. It is rather cold outdoors, but dry enough. Besides, I had a fur mantle to wrap about myself."

"And you saw no one?" Will asks her.

"No." Lady Mary smiles then. "Unless you mean that funny little old man."

"Describe him." Lady Mary describes Isaac ben Mordecai to the very inch.

"He passed me as I went out. I thought it odd that Henry had no guard on his door, but he seemed harmless enough."

"Did you pass anyone else?"

"Only in the outer court. I had the misfortune to meet with Uncle Norfolk. He tried to feel my … well, never mind what … but he was most unpleasant to me, as usual."

"Will he tell your sister about your meeting?" Will asks.

"Never. He wants her and Henry bedded and wedded, as soon as possible. It does not serve his purpose to upset her. Besides, I know where all the Howard family skeletons are buried., and he is wary of what I might know."

"Such knowledge is a two edged sword," Will tells her. "Who else did you see?"

"Charles Brandon was lounging about. He was hoping to trap Henry into a game of cards. The silly man is out of funds again. I asked him what game he would play, and he said '*Milk the Jew*'. Do you know it, Will?"

"A sad little game, my lady," Will says. "Did you see anyone further? Think hard, Lady Mary, for it is of great importance."

"I shall, for you, Will." She closes in again. "Henry is not the vigorous man he used to be. I do my duty, of course, but I long for a more… *robust* lover during these long, cold nights."

"I am to be married, this very day," says Will, with a touch of remorse in his voice.

"His Majesty is *still* married," Mary says, laughing. "Your little Spanish bride cannot satisfy you every night of the week, Will. Come to me at Esher, and I will broaden your outlook on life."

"My lady… the others you saw?"

"None of any import. A couple of servants, a guard at the outer court door, and that handsome friend of yours."

"My friend?"

"Percy's young fellow. Though he claims he is in King Henry's service now, because of your influence with Cromwell."

"Harry Cork. Yes, he is a good sort. What was he about?"

"Loitering about, like all of your Thomas Cromwell's young men do. They lean on walls and listen to idle chatter. Then they pass it on to your master, and he weaves it into useful fact. So, he was listening in to Norfolk shouting at me, and to Suffolk talking about hunting with Harry Percy's dark shadow."

"Sir Andrew Jennings, you mean?" Will thinks it odd how so many gentlemen come to be up so early, and find themselves about the court, even as a murder is being done.

"Yes, he was attached to Charles Brandon, rather like a barnacle to a ship's keel."

"Your seafaring knowledge impresses me." Will is making mental notes.

"And what was Lord Percy doing?"

"Percy? Why, now I come to think of it, I did not see him at all."

"Thank you, Lady Mary," Will Draper says. " You have been of great service. Master Cromwell has a couple of men about court, and they can escort you back to Esher, if you wish."

"Thank you, but no. Henry has gentlemen with tight lips who will take me. My sister Anne believes Thomas Cromwell is her man, and it will not do to disabuse her of so silly an idea." Then she kisses him. Before he can avoid it, her lips brush his. He is tempted to enfold her in his arms, but knows it might cost him his head. Instead, he pretends not to have noticed, and takes his leave, bowing low.

There is sweat on his brow. He considers what she has told him, and decides to confirm her story with her volatile uncle. The Duke of Norfolk is not a pleasant man, and he dislikes Thomas Cromwell. Then again, Will recalls, he dislikes everyone.

10   The Aristocrats

Norfolk is occupying a window seat in the outer court. He recognises Will, and beckons him to come over. Draper places his left hand on his sword hilt, removes his cap, and executes a smart bow to the old man.

"By God's holy virgin bride," Norfolk declares, "but I do like a man with military style. Come to me here Captain, and tell me what in Christ's bloody name is going on?"

"I have here, a warrant from the King," Will says, and Norfolk blanches. He stands up, then takes a small, backward step. Great men can have great falls, and he wonders what he has done to deserve this. Draper realises at once that the Duke of Norfolk has misunderstood the nature of the warrant. He holds the paper out for further examination.

"Pray be at your ease, my dear Lord," he says to the rattled aristocrat. "It is not that kind of a warrant. God spare me from ever having to serve such a thing on your grace!" He has hit just the right note. Norfolk likes to be adored as a great man, and believes that common folk love him for his good breeding.

"I wonder what Thomas Cromwell would do if he ever had to arrest me," he says. "Shit himself?"

"No sir. He would obey the King," Will says. "First, he would make sure the warrant was legally drawn up, then he would send a messenger, asking when he might call to arrest you. Your Lordship would be well advised to reply from France, or the Netherlands."

Norfolk smiles at this. The soldier has some brains as well as military skills. Reply from France indeed! He laughs, loud enough for everyone in the great hall to turn and stare.

"I don't much care for the life of a pauper in a foreign land," he says, once his laughter subsides.

"Talk to Master Cromwell, my Lord," Will replies. "Let him lodge part of your wealth with our contacts in Paris, or Florence. They say both cities are beautiful places to live."

"I shall do as you suggest, young man." Norfolk is in a good mood now, ready to be spoken to. Will clears his throat.

"I spoke with Lady Mary Boleyn just now."

"The shameful slut. I should have her

sent back to France. She could practice her Magdalene ways on the French King." Norfolk is not a forgiving man.

"She claims you told her off this morning," Will says. "Is that so, my Lord?"

"Damn me, but I certainly did." Norfolk preens himself, and likes it that he can be rude to whomsoever he pleases. "I told her to get her tight little *putain* arse back to Esher, and to stop interfering in her poor sister's wedding plans."

"The King is still wed to Katherine," Will says. "Might not that delay things somewhat, My Lord?"

"She tells me that Cromwell is her creature now, and promises to sort everything out. Katherine will go to a nunnery," Norfolk says, "and my niece, Anne, will be Queen of England."

"Do you recall the time, sir?" Will asks.

"Time?" Norfolk has only a vague idea of time. He often forgets the day, and seldom knows the hour. It is enough that his servants know when to wake him, when to dress him, and when to feed him. "You must ask Charles Brandon about that. That stupid upstart, Suffolk, declares the hour with boring regularity. It is as if he owns time itself."

"I see." Will has no idea what the Duke of Norfolk is talking about. "You arrived early then?"

"I did."

"Why?"

"Why not?"

"My Lord, I must press you on this point. It is a matter of the King's safety."

"What? Oh, I see. No, no I do not see, actually. Never mind. Not important… what? I fled from home early because my infernal wife, Lady Elizabeth, was pressing me for… certain rights due to her… of a vaguely conjugal nature."

"She drove you out of your bed with these … demands?" Will asks, uncertain if he is not being taken for a fool.

"Yes, that is it, my lad." Norfolk confirms. "Why spend my strength on a brood mare, when there are younger, more willing, fillies to be mounted, eh?"

"So you came to court instead?" Will cannot help but sound unbelieving.

"You have obviously not met my wife, young man," Norfolk says to him. "She bred well enough, but time has not been her friend. Though still handsome in stature, and fair enough in face, I find her to be quite repugnant to me. She is ugly to me, sir, and her temper is foul. If must be, I would flee to far off Cathay, rather than sate her insistent passions."

Will Draper commiserates, bows, and takes his leave. The Duke of Norfolk is afraid of his own wife. Cromwell will want that for his file on Tom Howard. The great duke has been sitting on a window sill since early morning, rather than go home, and pleasure her, as any good husband would.

"Hold there, you damnable rogue, what is your business!" Will turns, hand slipping towards his sword hilt. It is only Harry Cork, affecting an officious and booming voice. He laughs, and throws out a hand to clasp. "Steady on there, Will, I don't want to fight you again!"

"Harry Cork." Will smiles at the open faced young man. "I see you have emulated a cat, and landed on your feet."

"Thanks to you, my dear friend," Harry replies, and pats the fine linen of his new, royal livery. "You vouched for me with Master Cromwell, just like you promised."

"You sent me to him, remember?" Will says. "It was a good deed you did me, Harry. I knew my master would help you out. He is a generous soul to those he takes a liking to."

"He placed me here, in court," young Cork explains. "I am a fetch and carry boy, for now, but the pay is fair, and prospects are looking rather good. Master Cromwell also sends me a small weekly stipend, and he asks only that I keep my eyes and ears open on his behalf."

"And have you?" Will takes Cork by the elbow, and leads him off into a quieter corner. "Do you know what is afoot?"

"I know that King Henry was dealing with a famous Jew banker." Cork looks around, as if the walls are listening. "The man is dead. Murdered, they say."

"Do 'they' happen to say by whom?" Will is alarmed that the secret is being gossiped about. Harry Cork shrugs his shoulders. Every single person will tell you different. It depends on who you are for.

"Master Cromwell's name is touted about. But he is behind everything, if you listen to the silly talk. Thomas Cromwell killed the Jew so he could steal his pretty daughter for his harem. What do you say to that nonsense, my friend?"

"It is his grand daughter who is taken into Cromwell's home, but it is I who am to be her husband." Will sees there are more lies than truths abroad. "We were to be wed today."

"I'm sorry for that," Harry Cork says, sincerely. "I would not have you kept from your bride any longer than necessary. The fact is, Will, that most think the poor man angered the King, and he had him done away with."

"In the King's own rooms?" Will shakes his head. "Hardly likely, is it, Harry?"

"Hardly... no. It is only a silly rumour." Harry Cork replies. "You know about Charles Brandon, of course?"

"I know the earl is a born fool, and a waster of money, and a rank womaniser," Will Draper says. "Is that enough, my friend, or is there more to him?"

"He has been spending all of his borrowed money on a slip of a girl in Norwich," Cork reveals. "At home, his wife is ill and, some say, close to death. Mary is the King's dearly beloved younger sister. The older one, Margaret, is Queen of Scots... though widowed just now."

"Let me take a wild guess," Will says with dry humour. "Henry has found out about Brandon's wandering desires."

"He heard it from Harry Percy, who is a relative of the young girl in Norwich,"

Cork explains. "He is not keen on the Earl of Suffolk tupping a Percy lamb. The King, it is said, roared like a wounded beast at the news. Then he says to one of his guards, '*Bring me Brandon, and I will rip out his heart*'. I could hear him clear down the great long corridor!"

"Then Suffolk is also out of favour," Will says, and furrows his brow in thought. Surely, the thing to do is flee the court, rather than come calling, he thinks. "Why then does he chance coming to court?" he asks his friend, who can only shrug.

"You must ask him that," Harry Cork replies. "Perhaps he owes money to the J… I mean your… relative. He is perhaps here to ask for more time, and Master Isaac refuses his request. They argue back and forth, and Charles Brandon, desperate for want of gold, takes out his knife, and plunges it into the poor fellow's heart. It would be an unplanned killing, of course… but still murder."

"Perhaps, but again, most unlikely." Will adds these snippets to his bank of knowledge. "Keep on your toes, Harry. I must know of anything unusual that occurs. Any strange visitors to court, or sudden attempted departures. You understand?"

"I do. Master Cromwell has put you in charge of a murder investigation, and you have the King's writ in your hand. Speak to Suffolk, my friend. He was curled up in a corner earlier, fiddling with his new toy. Ask him about Isaac, and ask him why he dares to show his face in court when Henry wants his blood."

"I will, Harry. Keep yourself safe." Will means it. There is a killer in court, and he might well strike again. He strolls down the long corridor, until he comes upon a bundle of crumpled, malodorous, clothing that turns out to be none other than Charles Brandon, the out of favour Earl of Suffolk.

Poor Suffolk has not changed his clothes for three or four days, and his cheeks are unshaven, and rough. Will Draper thinks he has been sleeping under the stars, in fear of stopping in one place too long, lest Henry's vengeful men take him, and put him in irons.

"Good day, my Lord." Will bows. The duke looks out of bleary eyes, and thinks he knows this man. There is something about the bold way he stands that is familiar. He struggles to raise himself to his feet, and Will smells the stench of strong drink on him. He returns Will's slight bow, his hand resting on his sword hilt.

"And to you, sir. Have you been named to me before? I think we have, perhaps, met somewhere else. At Madam Larue's establishment, perhaps? Her new tarts are quite…"

"No sir, it was here," Will replies. "I brought a message to the King, saying that Cardinal Wolsey was dead, in Leicester."

"Ah, I gave you a purse in reward," Charles Brandon says, wishing he had it now. "Have you found work here then? You have soldiered in Ireland too, I recall."

"Yes, my Lord. Captain Will Draper, at your service. I am looking into certain matters for His Majesty, and find I must ask you some questions." He shows his paper. Suffolk struggles to read the words. He is a gentleman, and the skill was never much needed.

"Ask what you may," Suffolk says. "I am the King's closest friend, and, despite our current quarrel, I love him dearly, and Hal loves me too. He will forgive me my stupid error, and we shall be reunited in friendship."

"Can you tell me when you came to court?" Will asks.

"This morning, of course. I rode all

night to get here. Henry likes to play tennis, you see, and I hoped to rekindle his love of me during a furious game or two. Do you know … I have never managed to beat him, in twenty three years of play."

"A wise move, My Lord. I suggest you defer to the King in everything, until his temper cools. Tell him you have been cruelly slandered by Harry Percy, and are still a faithful, and loving husband to his dear sister Mary."

"Harry Percy?" Suffolk draws himself up to his full height. At six feet, he is a mere scrap shorter than Henry. "That worthless young dog went to Henry, behind my back…. but why?"

"The girl in question is some sort of a cousin of his," Will explains. "Deny everything. Ask… no, insist that the King appoints Thomas Cromwell to investigate the claims. He will find you to be completely innocent, and this overly willing girl will be re-settled somewhere far away. Perhaps Lord Percy might keep her … as a penance for his sins?"

"Of course. You are one of Cromwell's clever young men. I remember now." Suffolk seems, all at once, to be more cheerful. Cromwell has the King's ear, and will stop Henry from putting a fresh head atop the city gates. Then he thinks… what if Cromwell's price is too high to pay?

"What will your master want in return, Captain Draper?"

"Friendship, my lord," Will tells him, honestly. "When Henry asks what you think about a certain policy, tell him you agree with Thomas Cromwell. If he should ask who he might appoint to a high office, tell him Cromwell will have the ideal person. Do this for him, and my master will see to it that those concerned, forget to call in the interest on your unfortunate debts."

"He is the coming man," Suffolk says.

"That's the idea, my Lord." Will smiles encouragingly. "Now, what time did you say you came here?"

"A quarter hour from eight," the Duke of Suffolk says. "My Lord Norfolk arrived five minutes later. He is hiding from his licentious wife again. Perhaps you can have her sent away to a nunnery, or find her work in a bawdy house? Poor old Norfolk would kiss you, if you made him a free man again."

"And when did Percy turn up?"

"The Duke of Northumberland is

staying with a cousin just outside the city walls. He came in at five minutes after eight, with Sir Andrew Jennings in tow. He is a bad bastard, and no mistake."

"Percy?" asks Will.

"No, though he is a most loathsome cur. I mean that swine, Drew Jennings. He fawns and bows, like a French gentleman, but inside, the very devil is at play. Do you not know the tales about him, Captain Draper?"

"Enlighten me, my Lord." Will sits down beside the Duke of Suffolk in his window sill, and prepares to listen to some useful gossip.

*

Harry Cork has only light duties, and finds himself with enough spare time to loiter close to the Duke of Norfolk, who has fallen into conversation with another man. The two speak in lowered voices, and he is hard pressed to overhear their conversation. The words 'Jew' and 'money' figure often in their parlay, and Cork makes a mental note to speak with Will Draper again.

His position at court depends on Thomas Cromwell, and the young captain seems to have the great man's ear. If he can collect together enough scraps of gossip, he might well find himself rising up the slippery pole.

"Bastard!" Norfolk says, and cuffs his visitor hard across the head. "I do not want excuses... you toad. If the Jew is dead, find me a Lombard, and be quick about it!"

"At once, sir," the other man says, and skulks away to do as he is bid.

*

Suffolk loves to gossip, and likes nothing more than to find a ready listener, who does not know the old story. He tells Will that he must go back to 1520. Jennings was not a knight back then, he explains with relish. He was a tax collector for Northumberland.

"Not Harry Percy, God rot him with stinking pox, but his father, the old Duke. Black Hal they used to call the old man." the Duke of Suffolk explains. "The old man used to say Drew Jennings was the best tax collector he ever knew. The method is simple enough. I have tax collectors on my estates. They evaluate a man, and levy a tax on him. I usually charge a penny an acre, and a tithe of all cattle, sheep and wool."

"And Jennings was good at this?"

"Excellent, more like. If my tenant fails to pay, we give him another month or two. Then we threaten them. As a last resort, I take their land back, and give it to a worthier tenant. This is a time consuming business, and often ends with me losing out in some way. Andrew Jennings collected every penny due, and always on time."

"How?" Will asks.

"The story goes that he picks a village, waits 'til nightfall, then sets light to an outbuilding. Then he rides in, the next day, and says, next time, it will be your houses. The word gets around, and they pay."

"Very nice. And how does that make him so evil?"

"One day, an elder of this poxy village… some shit hole near Durham, I think… stands up to Jennings. He says he will appeal to the Duke, or even petition the King for justice. Drew Jennings jumps from his horse as the man turns away, and stabs him thus!" Suffolk makes a dramatic movement with his hand. "Then, he orders all the male relatives of the man to be rounded up. He fears they might seek vengeance, you see… and he locks them in a barn, and sets it alight."

"Dear Christ." Will is appalled.

"Nine dead," Suffolk says. "The next

day, the man's wife comes to ask how the women folk shall live, with their men dead. Jennings, has a fine solution. He takes the prettiest of the three daughters, and ravishes her in front of the mother. Then he auctions off the rest to the local soldiery, who use them as barracks whores. The violated daughter was twelve years old."

"The stinking animal," Will snaps.

"When Black Hal died, and young Harry Percy became the new Duke of Northumberland, it is said that he went in search of Drew Jennings. Now the swine is knighted, and does everything evil that the Percy bastard desires."

"A terrible story, my lord. Which leads me to ask, how did you know the time so precisely?"

"Ah, yes. My new toy from Italy." He brandishes his wrist, to show a casket, half the size of a closed fist strapped to it. "They call it a watch. For the sailors of Genoa use them to mark their watches when at sea."

Will is transfixed. Suffolk raises the lid, and displays a miniature clock dial, with a small, silver pin fixed at its centre. Charles Brandon has nothing short of a sundial on his wrist. The Duke loves to boast. He explains how he won it from the Genoese ambassador at the card table, and gives a demonstration.

"See," he says, turning himself to face the window. "One must catch the light from the sun. Today is not so good, but this morning, the sky was as clear as a young nun's conscience. You line it up, thus, and observe the shadow. By this method, you can tell the time to within a few minutes."

"Amazing, my Lord. Thank goodness I am not concerned with night timings. Or do you hold it to a candle?"

"Oh, would that work?" Will Draper can hardly contain his laughter. This is a tale for the Austin Friars breakfast table. The idea that Suffolk might go in search of a candle to read his miniature sundial by is just too rich for words.

"I think not, sir," Will tells him with a wry smile. "Do you recall any others out and about this morning?" It is a simple question, but the Duke of Suffolk frowns, as if he would rather be elsewhere at that precise moment.

"Like More, you mean?"

"Sir Thomas More was here?" Will asks.

"He was, but you have not heard that

from me. The new Lord Chancellor was up early… as was Stephen Gardiner, and Master Richard Rich. Then there was Lady Margaret Bulstrode, and her sister Jane. They are the mistresses of …well, anyone with the price, I suppose. Lovely girls. I had the pleasure of their company once, before I married of course. They are inseparable, even in the bed chamber."

The list is ever growing. Margaret and Jane Bulstrode, creeping away from someone's bed might be of use. Sir Thomas More, the sour faced Lord Chancellor, and his two cronies, in court at an ungodly hour, also gives him a path to follow. As he crosses a name off, more appear to take its place.

"Have I been of use, young man?" Charles Brandon, Duke of Suffolk, is keen for Henry to hear of his helpfulness. It might just be enough to stay his vengeful hand.

"Yes sir. You, and your wonderful *watcher machine* have thrown light where there was none." He is about to take his leave when it occurs to him that Suffolk is in a parlous condition. "When last we met, sir, you gave me a purse which you thought to be of coppers, as a small reward for my task. On opening it, I saw you had made a grave mistake, and given me silver instead. I have been hoping to see you again, so that I could rectify the matter. Here is the purse, sir."

Suffolk is speechless. The bag weighs heavy on his palm. It will enable him to eat, pay for the services of a good barber, and bribe his way in to the king's indoor tennis court. Once in Henry's company he can proceed to lose a few games, and butter the king up again. The forty silver shillings, given up so freely, will help him restore his credit at court, and allow him access to the monarch.

"Your honesty is commendable," he says, shaking Will's hand with vigour. "Please, mention to Master Cromwell that I might call on him soon. A man can never have enough good friends."

"He will be waiting, sir." Will bows himself away. He is doing sterling work for the banking interests of Thomas Cromwell, and has been carefully schooled into what to say, but he is no nearer finding the elusive killer of Isaac ben Mordecai.

He consults his mental list. It is best to separate the wheat from the chaff. The wheat are those who are almost certainly innocent, and once they are separated he shall better see the worrisome chaff in all their wicked splendour.

*

He goes in search of Sir Thomas More's offices which, he is told, are in the east end of the sprawling palace. The Lord Chancellor's men are distinctive in their livery, and the man himself is soon found.

"There is a young man outside, Sir Thomas," his servant says, dropping his voice to a whisper. "He has a document from the King, saying you *must* talk to him."

"Must?" More smiles. "Words can be interpreted in many ways, I will see this document for myself, and see if it is twistable to my own needs. Show the man in."

Will Draper has seen the Lord Chancellor before. He bows, and introduces himself. Sir Thomas holds out his hand for the warrant, and reads it through, twice.

"You are one of Cromwell's thugs," he says, curtly. "Why would King Henry give you such a catch all dispensation?"

"I am empowered to ask questions, sir, not answer them."

"Good Lord… you aren't Cromwell's son are you? You sound just like him, and no mistake. I once knew a young man who…"

"Your pardon, Sir Thomas, but the King is waiting for my report, and I do not wish to anger him further than is necessary," Will hints.

"Further?" More is disturbed by this reply. "Who is it that has angered the King?"

"Is that another question, sir?"

The Lord Chancellor laughs, and wonders if Will Draper is for turning. He would make a fine Lord Chancellor's man, and no mistake about it. No, he decides, Cromwell's people are completely loyal, if nothing else. More wonders if the king is angered with him already because he has allowed several Wolsey supporters slip away to France.

"The king is upset about Edwin Tunnock then?" he asks.

"Who, sir?" Will Draper has never heard the name, and cannot help but think the business of the royal court is too labyrinthine ever to completely understand.

"Never mind. Well, what do you want to know?"

"You were in the royal court at eight this morning," Will says. "Why was that, sir?"

"State business."

"And?"

"And not for your ears."

"I shall tell His Majesty what you say, sir. Perhaps he can ask you directly."

"You threaten so beautifully, young man. Tom Cromwell has done a fine job with you," Sir Thomas says. "I and two colleagues were hoping to see the King before he met with the Jew, Isaac ben Mordecai. I wished to deter His Highness from such an ill chosen path. England should not be mortgaged off to Christ Killers."

"You knew about the loan?"

"Half of England knows." More sees he must explain. "The King tells a close friend, who tells his mistress, who tells her maid, who tells me, who tells Stephen Gardiner, who then tells Richard Rich, who tells Thomas Cromwell... who tells nobody."

"Did you arrive together?" Will asks, but notes that this Rich fellow seems quite happy to play both sides for his own benefit.

"Yes. The King refused to speak with me so early, and insisted that we left him alone. He shouted at us through a locked door, would you believe? So, we came back here, to my suite of offices, and had a working breakfast."

Poor Gardiner and Rich, Will thinks.

It is known throughout England that the Lord Chancellor keeps a very poor table. He imagines the three, sharing gruel, and heels of stale bread.

"When did the other gentlemen leave?"

"Stephen Gardiner only stayed a few minutes, but Richard Rich helped me sort some letters until about ten. I find secretarial things for him, now and then. Now, may I finally ask a question?"

"You may, sir."

"Is my information correct? Is the Jew dead?"

"He is."

"God be praised," More says, smiling. "By whose hand?"

Will shrugs. More has taken Stephen Gardiner's alibi from him, and the list is hardly diminished at all.

"Where is Master Gardiner now?"

It is Sir Thomas More's turn to shrug. Let Tom Cromwell's man earn his pay and find the fellow for himself. With the Jewish moneylender now dead, Henry must reconcile himself with the Italian bankers, which will bring him back to the Pope. More is against all this silly talk of annulment, and wants the King back in the bed of Katherine of Aragon. England must stand firm against the Lutherans, he thinks, and remain a devoutly Roman Catholic country.

"Poor Stephen is a martyr to insomnia these days, and hardly ever sleeps," More says, conversationally. Then he thinks to make a sour faced jest. "Might he have killed your Jew whilst out sleep walking?"

"Thank you for your observations, Sir Thomas," Will says, but wants to leave the man with a sharp retort. "Did *you* sleep alone last night?"

"What?" Sir Thomas More is outraged. His views on fornication outside marriage are well known. "You dare impugn…"

"I impugn nothing, sir," Will snaps. "It is simply that had you been swiving the Bulstrode sisters last night you would have … all three of you … a most believable alibi!"

"Young man," More says with an indignant ring to his voice, "I am a married man… and as such… I obviously slept alone!"

11   The Dog Pit

Will Draper leaves the Lord Chancellor to his stately machinations, and goes in search of Stephen Gardiner, Principal Secretary to the King. He knows that Gardiner was, until recently, a devoted Wolsey man, and expects his full co-operation.

"What do you expect of me?" Gardiner asks, casually. He is sitting at a high stool in his Greys Inn law establishment. "I told Sir Thomas More he was an utter fool to try and obstruct the will of the King. We are in England, not Utopia, and different rules must apply."

"That is not my concern, sir. Master Cromwell has promised the king that…"

"Cromwell? Hah! Is the old scoundrel struggling to satisfy His Majesty these days? He and I were colleagues once, you know, but Wolsey set us at each others throats. Has he told you the story of how we quarrelled over the matter of William Tyndale? No, I see not from the look on your face. Did you not know your master is a dangerous heretic?"

"Then I am sure Sir Thomas More will gladly prosecute him for the crime,"

Will replies. He has heard of Tyndale, and his notorious English bible, and knows that a printed copy of it resides in his master's study. "The Lord Chancellor has a way of turning men from Satan, has he not? A turn of the rack, and the smell of roasting flesh."

"Tom More is a fool. He thinks himself to be safe, because of his great reputation," Gardiner says, then falls into silence. Cromwell's man has been handed an easy victory. "There, you may run off and tell Tom Cromwell that I dislike Thomas More. He will note it down in his big black book, and drop you a shilling for your trouble."

"I have no interest in the petty squabbles between two old fishwives, Master Gardiner." Will sees that this stings the man. He has scored a hit on England's second finest lawyer. "I want only an honest answer to all of my questions."

"Which are?"

"When did you leave Sir Thomas this morning?"

"About nine."

"He says sooner."

"Then, perhaps it was."

"Where were you between eight and nine?"

"With More for a little while, trying to get him to forbear from annoying Henry. Then, I went for a stroll in the gardens. They look so lovely at this time of year do you not think?"

"Did you pick any pretty blooms?" Will says. It is a stab in the dark, but stranger things happen, so he asks; "I hear that two lovely flowers were up and about early. The Lady Margaret Bulstrode, and Jane, her sister. You know them, sir?"

"That is a damned lie!"

"Your pardon, sir, but how do I lie?"

Stephen Gardiner is a man of letters, much admired for his cleverness, his honesty, and his religious nature. To better his career, he has taken holy orders, and renounced the sins of the flesh. He thinks this a formality only, and often seeks solace in the arms of a pretty woman or two.

"You seek to slur my character, Captain." Stephen Gardiner draws himself up, and turns, as if to cut Will dead.

"Better that than the suspicion of murder, Master Gardiner," Will says, and the man's back hunches, as if a knife has been driven between the shoulder blades. He turns back, his face suffused with horror.

"Then it is true. The Jew is really

dead?"

"Murdered, sir. I am looking for someone who cannot state where they were at nine o'clock."

"Dear Christ, young man, I am a politician, but I have also taken on holy orders," Gardiner tells him. "Think what you are asking me to confess to."

"Not so, sir." Will understands now. Stephen Gardiner is the kind of priest who cannot eschew the comforts of the flesh, and with two sisters at once! There is plainly more to the man than Will thinks. Lady Margaret and her sister will confirm who their bed partner was, and that he slipped away early to bring them a little gift of gold for their splendid efforts. Cromwell will love this. "I see nothing to be ashamed of. As a man of the church, it is only proper that you meet with these two Magdalene's, and try to dissuade them from their overtly carnal ways. Your job is to save souls, is it not?"

"What? Oh, I see. Yes. I sought them out to turn them back onto the right path." Gardiner is saved from embarrassment, and by a Cromwell man. He does not quite see why.

"The two young ladies will be questioned… in a day or two… and may be asked who they shared their favours with last night. Perhaps you might speak with them before then, and insist they name their latest lover."

"Oh, God." Gardiner's heart skips a beat. "Whatever do you mean?"

"I am *absolutely* sure they will name Harry Percy."

"They will? I mean, yes... they probably will."

"I know this might show Percy in a bad light with the King," Will explains, "but he is an unpleasant young man, and needs to be taken down a peg or two."

Stephen Gardiner smiles. Percy is no friend to him, and does nothing to help in the matter of Henry's annulment. He bows to Will, and searches his belt for his purse. Will Draper holds out a staying hand.

"No need, sir. Your innocence is clear to me. All I want in return is your friendship... for my master."

"You strike a hard bargain, Captain Draper," Gardiner says, "but we were friends once, you know."

"Master Cromwell is with you on the great matter of the King, and will seek your support, one day." Bishop Gardiner nods. He will be Thomas Cromwell's friend, as long as it helps the King, but he fears they will disagree over Tyndale, and says so.

"It is just a book, sir," Will says. "Few can read anyway, and a few words mumbled in English, rather than Latin will do no harm. Give Harry Percy a copy, and he will have his kitchen girls wrap fish in its sacred pages."

"Not all are as loutish as the Duke of Northumberland," Stephen Gardiner says. "There is a man who could do murder, without flinching."

"He is high on my list," Will replies. "Do you know his whereabouts, Master Gardiner?"

"What hour is it?"

"About six, sir."

"Then you must try the dog pits in Westminster," Stephen Gardiner says, his voice dripping with disdain. "He has the most barbaric of tastes, and enjoys watching animals rip each other apart."

*

So he does, the young soldier concludes. Will finds his quarry roistering at Jeb Huntley's famous dog pit. It is the best in London, and caters for both the gentry, and the aristocracy. Those in the know claim that Huntley uses the best fighting dogs in

England, and that he is as straight as any man can be.

"My Lord Percy?" Will bows, but keeps a wary eye on Sir Andrew Jennings, who sidles off to one side. Harry Percy, Duke of Northumberland, downs the cup of strong ale in his hand, and stares at the newcomer. The face is familiar, he thinks, but the long drinking sessions have befuddled his mind.

"What of it, fellow?" the duke asks.

"I have come from the King, to ask…"

"What does the old man want now?" Percy sneers. "He has my woman, and prates to me about the immorality of his marriage to Katherine. Shall I come and help him in his privy, or does he want to know how best he might mount his new filly?"

"Have a care," Sir Andrew Jennings urges, quietly. "This one is a Cromwell dog. I can smell them a mile off. You are the one we sent with news of Wolsey's death, aren't you?"

"I am, sir."

"That was a bad day's work. The King still bears a grudge against us for it. As if we'd knocked the old man on the head, our own selves," Drew Jennings says. "My

Lord Percy is presently in his cups, and so he speaks without thought."

"A dangerous occupation," Will replies.

"As is yours," Jennings says, smiling. "Messengers are a penny a dozen, and often end up floating in the river."

"Have a care of what you say, sir," Will tells him. "Read this before you decide to make of me an enemy." He holds out the warrant, and Jennings, his lips moving, reads it for Harry Percy.

"I see." The warrant is clear, and written so widely that it gives Will Draper enormous power. "What do you want of us?"

"Your whereabouts between eight and nine this morning."

"We were both in bed," Jennings says, smartly.

"Together?" Will asks, and raises a quizzical eyebrow.

Sir Andrew Jennings wants to draw his blade, and teach the man a sharp lesson. Instead, he laughs, and pats Percy on the back.

"Hear this, Harry? The ill bred lout thinks we make the beast together. I warrant you'd want a prettier face than mine."

"You were seen in court at eight."

Will catches Percy's desperate glance, and Jennings look back, mutely saying, keep quiet, I will tend to this fellow and his intrusive enquiries.

"By whom?" he asks.

"People. Several, and diverse, sir."

"You talk like a lawyer."

"I seek only the truth."

"My Lord Percy and I … cannot recall. Ah, here are the dogs."

Jennings turns his back on Will Draper, shielding him from his master. Two men appear, each holding a leashed beast. The animals are placed in the deep pit, and, as men cluster around, the dogs are released at one another in a frenzy of blood lust.

The crowd, who have backed one dog or the other, scream and push their way to the front. Will loses Percy for a moment, then sees him, standing alone. One of the dogs is on the other's back, its teeth sinking into its neck. The other twists about, and tries to rip open his enemy's flank. Flecks of blood spatter the watching mob.

Where is Jennings? Will remembers Suffolk's story, of how he fell on the farmer from behind. The hairs on his neck stand on end. He glances over his left shoulder, just in time to see the man moving onto him. He half turns, takes the man's wrist as he tries to push, and trips him as he lunges forward.

The look of fright on Jennings' face is there, frozen in a moment of time. Then he is gone, tumbling down into the deep pit. The crowd roar their appreciation as the frenzied dogs turn on this new intruder. Will steps back, even as Jennings' screams begin to tear through the air. The dogs owners will not let a gentleman die, of course. It is considered to be quite bad for business. They jump in the pit, with shouts and curses, and drive the dogs off their terrified, and lacerated, prey.

Outside, Will takes in a gulp of fresher air. He has never liked the smell of blood overly much, despite his previous profession. A young lad, little more than a child, sidles up to him and offers his virgin sister for a shilling. He sees that this is not a runner, so offers Will something else instead.

"Give us a penny, an' I'll tell you something," he says. Will is about to brush the child away, but there is that in his tone that makes him pause. He rummages in his purse, brings out some small coppers, and teases the child with them.

"Make it good, and I'll give you these." he says. The boy is hungry, and the money tempts him.

"Someone is following you." Will nods. He flips a penny to the boy. This is a story that must be paid for by the inch, he thinks.

"Who?" The boy smiles, and holds out his palm. Another penny is exchanged. He bites it. The time honoured method of testing the metal's worth shows the second coin to be as good as the first.

"Me."

"You? Clever lad. Who set you on to me?"

"A priest, sir. Is that worth another penny?"

"Only if you tell me everything," Will says. "I am one of the King's men, and to follow me may see you swinging on the gallows."

"I can't tell a tale with a rope around my neck, master." The boy is a smart one. "This priest is standing outside the *jakes* when I comes out. You get a lot of Godly sorts waiting around there. The public privy pit seems to attract their sort of trade."

"Their sort?"

"Sodomites, sir. Only this one just wants me to follow you about for the day." The boy smiles, knowingly. "I was getting tired of it, and thought I might get you to stay at Moll Deakins' whore house for an hour or two. She is a good sort, and does not overcharge for her services."

"Then she's not your sister?"

"Bless, no, sir. The gentlemen just find it more fun if they think they are tupping my sister. They get worked up, and tip me more copper."

"You are an enterprising lad. How were you meant to report to this priest?"

"I wasn't, sir. I was just meant to follow you, and warn you if any evil is afoot."

"You failed, young fellow."

"I never thought one of your own was going to do you harm," the boy replies. "I thought the priest meant some rough or other. I swear. I don't think that fellow will make another attempt. Not after the dogs have chewed on him for a while. I was fit to burst with laughing at your antics, sir."

"Do you have a name, child?"

"I do, but I don't want it written down, sir."

"It shall be between us. My word, as a gentleman." Will is intrigued. A boy as guardian angel?

"Adam Bright, if it please… and if it

don't. For that is all I have." The boy
pockets his coins. "Am I to carry on my
job?"

"Why not?" Will tells him. "The
priest has paid you for it, has he not? Trail
behind, and watch."

"I saw you come out of York Place,"
Adam says. "The guards will not let me
trespass there."

"Wait outside then. I can deal with
any I find within."

"Have a care, master. There ain't no
dog pits in the King's palaces."

True. Though there are some
dangerous creatures roaming the corridors, it
seems. A friendly priest, and a murderous tax
collector, Will thinks. It is a heady mix. At
that moment, Harry Percy, Earl of
Northumberland comes staggering out from
the dog pit, and throws up.

"Can I be of some assistance, My
Lord?"

"You again?" Percy looks like
warmed over death on a cold platter. "You
threw my man to the dogs ... you filthy
scoundrel!"

"Drew Jennings will heal, sir." Will
takes the Duke firmly by his elbow, and
moves him out of the road of a passing cart.

"You say the King stole your woman, My Lord. How so?"

"The Lady Anne, of course."

"Have a care. Your tongue will lose you your head, sir. Jennings was right to silence you when he did."

"My lovely Anne. We were betrothed, you know. She pledged herself to me before a priest. Then that scurrilous bastard Wolsey became involved. I told him... I said... we are one, and the man laughed in my face. Then he gets to his feet, and roars for Cromwell. Of course, that was that. You don't cross Thomas Cromwell, do you?"

"What happened?" Will bites his tongue. He does not wish to know. Every word is treasonable, and likely to ruin anyone touched by the affair.

"Tom Cromwell wasn't so high and mighty back then," Percy says. "He took me by the throat, and swore he would rip it out if I uttered another word. Then he had me taken back to Northumberland, where my father... rot his soul in hellfire... told me to marry another."

"This was before the King looked on Lady Anne with the royal favour?"

"Yes. Many others were keen on

her… like the poet fellow… Wyatt, but I was considered far too grand for her back then. Her father tried to outdo Wolsey, and make the marriage hold, but old Boleyn is a craven coward at heart. The cardinal simply snapped his fingers, and Tom Cromwell saw him off. He called Wolsey a bloody butcher's boy, and Cromwell struck him to the ground, and then he kicked his scrawny arse, all the way back to Norfolk."

"Enough of this scurrilous chatter, sir. You really must hold your tongue," Will Draper insists. He is a Cromwell man, but does not want to become privy to too many secrets. That is for his master to risk, not he.

"Whilst I still have it?" Percy pulls away, and sets off down the filth strewn street. "Have a care, Cromwell's cur, for he has made too many enemies to live much longer."

Will shakes his head. It is easy to see why his master surrounds himself with loyal young men. Men who would die for his sake. Percy hates him, and George Boleyn hates him for his father's sake. It is a wonder that it is Isaac who is dead, when others seem to have so many enemies. He signals to Adam Bright. The boy runs over to him.

"Sir?"

"You see that gentleman?"

"Lord Percy, sir?"

"You know him?"

"A regular with the working girls I run errands for, sir." Adam grins. "They say he often has trouble with his lordly pintle, but pays never the less."

"I see. Fall in with him, and guide him to a nice clean house, where he can be with a nice clean girl. See he is kept out of harms way."

"It will take silver, sir."

"Here." Two silver shillings change hands, and the child runs off, after the third most powerful man in England. There, Will thinks, that is Percy out of the way for a while. May God teach him to keep his chattering mouth shut, henceforth.

*

"Any news, brother?" Miriam's eyes are puffed, and red with tears. She places a hand on Moshe's forearm.

"Will is abroad, trying to uncover the villain."

"You should be by his side."

"I am torn, sister," Moshe replies. He wants to help his soon to be brother in law, but fears to leave his sister alone. Jew killers seldom stop at one, and he loves her too much to risk her life.

"I am safe in Austin Friars," Miriam says. "These are good people, and treat me very well." Moshe ben Mordecai, now Morden, sees the truth of this. He himself has been absorbed into the household without a murmur of dissent. The rest of Cromwell's young men have taken to calling him 'Mush' and bait him with thick slices of pork at breakfast. It is good natured banter, and he sees that they will do anything to help one another.

"I'll seek your Will out, sister," he agrees, "but only if you swear not to leave the grounds of Austin Friars without me by your side."

"On the bible?" she says, and they both smile at this. A change of surname cannot change over three thousand years of Hebraic tribal history.

"The English one that Master Thomas has under his bed," Moshe replies. "The new Gospel according to Tyndale will tear this poor country apart, sister."

"Ah, Mush, there you are," Rafe steps from behind a half open door. "Not thinking of going out, are you?"

"My sister thinks Will might have some need me."

"I'll come along… for the company."
Rafe has already buckled on his sword, and
is stuffing a loaded pistol into his belt.

"No need," the young Jew answers.
"I can take care of myself thank you, Rafe."

"And Richard will come too," Rafe
Sadler continues, ignoring his   young
friend's protestations. "I dare say Barnaby
Fowler fancies a stroll with us also."

"This is becoming something of a
war party, Rafe." Moshe says to the older
man. Rafe Sadler shrugs at this, and pushes a
second knife into his belt.

"Who strikes one, strikes us all,
Mush. The master says that, and we believe
it to be so. It is a goodly creed to follow. If
there is a Jew killer at large, then we are *all*
Jews, until further notice."

"Thank you," Moshe bows. "It will
be an honour, sir. We might have a better
chance of finding Will mob handed."

"Fiddle sticks," Rafe says. "We have
a hundred men stationed all over London.
Once word is out, we will have our man run
to earth in mere moments."

"God's speed," Miriam tells them.
There is only one God, in her book,
whatever men call Him. "And Moshe, I beg
of you to keep your temper under control …

should you find out the identity of our grandfather's murderer."

"Of course," Moshe says, but his fingers are crossed tightly behind his back. His history stretches back over four millennia, and is essentially tribal. The God of Abraham is not known for either his leniency, or for his forgiveness, and his chosen people have learned to understand their allotted place in the modern world. The Jews are hated and reviled across Europe, and they have no right to either law, or human justice in English eyes. So, he must make his own laws, and dispense his own justice.

Moshe has but one thought in his mind. Strike me and mine, and I will strike back, tenfold. Whether with the sword, or through more devious, fiscal means, the ben Mordecai family will be avenged.

"Shall we?" Rafe says, and the two comrades stroll out into the frost covered courtyard. Barnaby Fowler and Richard Cromwell are waiting for them, and each is more heavily armed than a Spanish conquistador. Richard is over six feet two inches tall, as broad as a prize winning bull, and eager for a scrap.

"Come, young Mush," he bellows,

"and let us find ourselves a culprit to gut."

"After a fair trial," Barnaby Fowler puts in. "After all… the law is the law!"

The small hunting party go forth into the stews of London, intent on finding their comrade, and running down the killer of Isaac ben Mordecai. They succeed in their first aim, finding Will Draper with ease, but the second objective is harder to gain. They find their comrade to be already back at court, and settle down to keep a close eye on him.

They feel unable to return to Austin Friars without the guilty party revealed, so resolve to shadow their comrade until the deed is accomplished. Looking for a murderer can be a dangerous pastime, and should be attempted only with help.

A Hue and cry, it seems, is not the way about things, and they must leave the solving of the case to Will Draper and his sharper mind. It will be for them to crack any heads that need cracking, and fighting any who wish to oppose their master, or threaten Austin Friars.

12   The Cardinal's Cook

Will Draper has been sitting in a chair all night. His mind is full of tiny scraps of knowledge, each jostling for position. His list of suspects is still long, for great men do not soil their own hands, if they can avoid it. Sir Thomas More is, theoretically, the most powerful commoner in England, and can bid a man's death with a stroke of the quill, but why do it so secretively? He could unmask a Jew, and have him burnt at the stake in the blink of an eye, and the king would have to stand idly by.

Charles Brandon, Earl of Suffolk owed the victim money, but is more likely to curl up in a corner, feeling sorry for himself than to drive home a dagger. Then again, he is friend to old Norfolk, and the Duke of Norfolk knows no restraints. Tom Howard's blood line is bested by none, and he knows it. If a man stands in his way, then Norfolk will strike like a startled viper.

Why though? Norfolk might owe money, but it is of no consequence. No court in the land will find against him, if they value their own skins. Perhaps Isaac has transgressed in another way? What if it is political? What if the Lombard bankers wished Isaac out of the way, so as to clear their own path back? Will ponders these things into the wee small hours.

Sir Thomas More is political too, of course. He is a true Catholic, and cannot suffer another creed. He might wish the loan to fail, if only to bring King Henry back to Pope Clement again. Will imagines the two great men, Henry and Clement, kissing one another's hands, but it is not an easy image to picture.

And tall, spare, Stephen Gardiner is another enigma. The man is an ordained clergyman, yet lets him know he has been with two women of loose morals for an alibi. Is he buying his innocence from a murder charge by letting his seeming moral turpitude show?

Then there is Harry Percy, Duke of Northumberland, by the Grace of God. Henry is angry with him, because he handled the Wolsey arrest so badly. He should be as far from court as he can manage, until the storm dies down. He and the Duke of Suffolk are a pair cast from the same mould, though one is far more likeable than the other.

Circles within circles. Will Draper begins to wonder if he is the man for this job at all. Then it is dawn, and he opens the door to his room at court to find a pile of snoring young men outside. He sticks out a boot, and nudges a black clothed thigh.

"Good morning Rafe... Richard... Mush... and who is that at the bottom of this undignified pile?... ah...my dear Barnaby. Sleep well, my friends?"

They struggle to their feet, smooth out crumpled black livery, and bow good mornings to their friend. It is a full day since the murder, and Henry is known to be an impatient monarch. If Will takes too long, the King of England will pluck a name from the hat at random, and hang the wrong man.

"We are here as bodyguards," Moshe says. "What can we do to help?"

"Disperse throughout the Court. Listen to every dark whisper, in every dark corner," Will says. He wants the gossip. Amongst the hundred silly stories told, there will be a few threads of truth. "I must question certain folk today, without observation."

"Did you not speak with every suspect person yesterday?" Rafe asks. More questions will mean more upset, and might bring danger knocking at all their doors.

"I am done with all these suspects. I

can make a case against each one," Will says. "Suffolk this, Norfolk that, and Percy the other. No, my friends, now I must talk to witnesses."

"Witnesses?" Richard Cromwell says, rubbing his eyes. He is a big, bear of a man, and the blood takes a little longer to reach his brain in a morning.

"I thought there were none," Barnaby says.

"Not eye witnesses," Will Draper tells them. It is a new thought he has. It came with the dawn, and will not leave him be. York Place is a silent witness, and must surrender her secrets to him. "I think the murder was planned, and I think the seeds of the crime were sewn in the past."

"Whose past?" Moshe asks.

"York Place's past," Will Draper says. "The old secrets of York Place will reveal the truth to me. I must go down to the kitchens."

"Ah, breakfast!" Richard is now fully awake. "Perhaps they will feed us all, if we show them the King's warrant? A man cannot run down murderers on an empty stomach."

"Sleep well, Will?" It is Harry Cork. He is suddenly amongst them, holding a bowl of rose water. "For the Lady Mary's room. It seems the king was afraid of nightmares, and needs must have a dainty hand to hold in the dark. Mary dabs it on her wrists, and any other place Henry might wish to kiss."

"Rose petals?" It is January. Will is not a gardening man, but the bushes are all bare in the gardens. "Where do they come from?"

Harry Cork shrugs. They simply appear. Like the ice in summer, or cucumbers out of season. Someone says 'Here, take this, fellow' and he takes it. Is it important? They look at one another. It is a mystery, but not one that seems to touch on the murder. Will is not so sure about this, and frowns at the innocent looking bowl.

"Do you put rose petal water in all the rooms, Harry?" Will does not know why he asks, but it suddenly seems to be important. His friend frowns back at him at him, as if he is losing some portion of his wits.

"Not all," he replies. "Mostly in the King's private quarters, and the rooms of any favoured guests."

"Like Lady Mary?"

"Amongst others," Harry tells him,

dropping his voice. "Henry has an eye for the pretty ones. They say he makes up for Lady Anne's coolness towards him by ravishing her ladies in waiting at every opportunity. It is said his royal member is quite prodigious."

"You do well to whisper such a disgraceful thing, Harry," Will says, who thinks it is a rumour most probably put about by the king himself. "We must not detain you any longer. The Lady Mary Boleyn will have great need of her rose petal water."

Harry Cork leaves, and Barnaby Fowler chuckles in an unpleasant way, then makes an odd quacking noise. Will Draper is astonished. He turns to him and asks why.

"One of Master Cromwell's lame ducks," Barnaby Fowler says, shrugging his shoulders. "I thought my impersonation to be most accurate, my friend."

"I don't understand." Will's voice has hardened.

"Barnaby means no slight against your friend, Will," Rafe Sadler says, soothingly. "It is just the master's way. If he takes to you, there is nothing he will not do for you. You become one of his young men, and your future is assured. I offer you up as a prime example of this. If he is not impressed at all… well, he acts otherwise. He does not like to turn anyone away, you see."

"Speak plain," Will says.

"Your friend, Harry Cork, is judged as simply not good enough for Master Cromwell's service, but he is your friend, and so the master takes pity on the poor thing. He declines to take Harry on, but recommends him to the king's service instead. Henry is satisfied. The King thinks he has taken on one of Wolsey's best young men, you see. Master Cork is so pleased, he fails to see he has been rejected by the better employer."

"Poor Harry Cork. He thinks he is Thomas Cromwell's secret eyes and ears in the king's court," Will says. "He did me a service I will find it hard ever to repay."

"No harm done," Rafe replies. "If he wishes to pass on any bits of tittle tattle, Master Cromwell will thank him, and drop a few silver coins in his hand for his trouble. The simple truth is that we know what Harry Cork knows, before even poor Harry Cork knows it!"

*

The kitchens at York Place are astounding. Designed and built to Cardinal Wolsey's strict desires, they are big enough to feed half of London. They contain all the most modern equipment, and are staffed by over a hundred trained men. There are butchers, sauce makers, specialists in cooking fowl, pie bakers, pot cleaners, spit turners, servant boys, bellows tenders, firewood fetchers, basting boys, dish washers, pastry makers, and assistant cooks. The huge spits work around the clock, and take two boys apiece to keep them turning. As one boy tires, he is replaced by another, fresher one. Each day, the butchers slaughter and dismember twenty sheep, fifty pigs, and whole flocks of pigeons, quail, ducks, geese, and swans.

The junior members of the staff are set to salting pork, curing fish and beef carcasses, and rendering great slabs of animal fat down into lard. The sauce makers have each served a year in the French court, discovering the secrets of Cathay spices, and Indian condiments, as well as the hundred ways to use creams in sauces. They are above the mundane peeling, pounding and roasting, and sit, like alchemists, mixing their delicious nostrums with which to beguile the king and his hungry royal court.

There are even two musicians in the great kitchen. Their job is to stroll amongst the workers, playing merry tunes on their flutes, or beating a rhythm on small snare drums, to keep the cooks at their multitudinous range of tasks.

Of them all, these cooks claim to be the most important. There are a dozen men, again trained in the French method, and overseen by Wat Turner, the master cook. He is of truly amazing girth, and it is said that no dish leaves his kitchen, unless he first samples it. In a competition against the French King's man, he won the prize purse by swallowing down sixty live oysters in one sitting, washed down with a half gallon of the strongest ale.

Cardinal Wolsey admired the man enough to pay him more than any other cook in London, and enjoyed his fine cooking, almost to the last. To taste everything was a huge task, and ensured nothing tainted ever got through. Other kitchens could not match his skill, and great men often tried to buy his services from the gourmet inclined cardinal. Turner wanted to go north with his master at the end, but Wolsey had refused, saying he must serve the house, rather than the man.

"Now, there was a real gentleman," Wat Turner says, when Will asks. "I was with Wolsey from the age of nine. I built this kitchen for him, and never knew a kinder man. God rest his poor, betrayed soul." He crosses himself fervently, and Will Draper copies the motion, muttering an appropriate amen.

"Master Cromwell speaks highly of him, still."

"Aye, and to the king's face," the old cook says with open admiration. "No one loved his master as much as Tom Cromwell did Cardinal Wolsey. He drops in, now and then, to exchange any new recipes. His cook is *almost* my equal. I trained him myself, so no surprise there, I think. What can I do for you, my good sir?"

"I am seeking history, Master Turner. Can you tell me about the time before King Henry took over York Place?"

"Stole it, more like." The cook is very confident of his position. Even a king will not chop the head off so talented a man. "Cardinal Wolsey was a good … no… an almost saintly man. King Henry was poisoned against him, by lesser folk. I look no further for the apportionment of blame than the damnable Boleyn family. Though it must be said that Harry, the Lord Percy, hated poor Cardinal Wolsey with a vengeance too."

"And what about the Duke of Norfolk?" Will Draper prompts.

"Yes, Norfolk wanted him dead also, and he finally got his evil, misbegotten way," Turner says, "but who can run England now, sir? Answer me that, if you can. It is too great a task, even for dear old Tom Cromwell, and his young men. Oh, how this great house rang with joy when Cromwell and his boys came a calling. He would come in, with his arms full of cherries, apples and pears, and demand I make them into dishes for the cardinal. It was he who suggested the idea about the red roses."

"The roses?" There it is again, Will thinks. Why do these damned rose petals stick in my mind so?

"Master Cromwell suggested we pot some in good, well manured soil, and keep them close to the warm hearths. They flower right through from September to March that way. The boys take the fallen petals and float them in the wash bowls, to help the fine ladies stink a little less. I dare say Mary Boleyn uses her fair share."

"Ah, I see." Will smiles at the simple solution to a small, nagging riddle. "My master is a wily one, and no doubt."

"Like a fox, Though he always made enough noise to warn my old master of his coming, did Cromwell. He was a common born lad, right enough… who isn't… but he really understood."

"About the women?" Will has an idea, and knows only below stairs knowledge will do now. His arrow is only slightly off target.

"Not women, sir. Bless my soul, the cardinal was not one for any rampant carnality," Wat Turner says. "It was just the one. A fine, well upholstered lady, sir, even if not of very good birth. The dear old rascal kept her in an adjoining room, whenever he was at York Place. 'Feed her up well, Master Wat' he would say to me. Then, when any important folk called, he would slip her away from sight."

"Like magic, eh?" Will laughs at the idea of the cardinal's voluptuous bed partner vanishing from sight. "The cardinal knew how to juggle his public and private life, I see."

"He did sir, and so clever about it too. Why, even now, this house refuses to give up her secrets."

"Tell me them, Master Turner," Will says. "I am in search of a murderer, and it is possible that you have the key."

"I sir?"

"You sir." Will draws the cook off to one side and begins to question him in earnest. Rafe, Richard and Barnaby are lusting after a huge game pie, which is cooling on one of the vast oak tables. They remember the Wolsey days, and his casual generosity. How he was as likely to drop a pie into your hand, as a silver coin. Be generous, and you will be repaid, if only in Heaven, he would say.

"What is Will Draper up to?" Barnaby Fowler asks. Rafe shrugs his shoulders, as if that will explain all. It is an odd feeling not to be the leader for once.

"He's a deep one," says Richard Cromwell. "Like our master. A man might drown in his mind."

"Well said, cousin," Rafe Sadler says, glancing casually about the huge, bustling room. With so much going on, anything might happen, unobserved. "Will this poor orphan of a pie fit under your doublet?"

"Come," Will says, returning to the small band. "I am done here." They leave, and Wat Turner, master of the king's kitchens, stands with his hands on his broad

broad hips, and curses like a soldier. The two foot long game pie, left cooling on the table, has gone.

*

"Did you find anything out from the cook?" Rafe says, through a mouthful of pie. The crust is light and crisp, whilst the blend of venison, hare, and wild duck meat, is fit for any King of England.

"I did," Will says. He takes out his knife, and cuts himself a thick slice. He has not eaten since the day before, and he is light headed with thinking. "The man was here with Cardinal Wolsey, from the start. He knows things that he does not even know he knows."

"See, deep, just as I said," Richard says, and belches. He is on his third large portion, and is already wondering what he will find to eat for dinner. Barnaby has left them, having to attend Lincolns Inn over a legal matter for their master, but has hid his slice under his cap.

"Hush, Richard." Rafe leans forward, conspiratorially. "What is it, Will? What do you know."

"Everything… and nothing." Will swallows a bite, and savours the taste. "I know how it was done, and I think I know who did it but, for the love of Christ, I do not understand the motivation."

"Do we need to?" Moshe says. He cannot eat the pie, unless its contents have been prepared ritually. "Give me a name, and I will slit his throat."

"No, that is the last thing we must do. I need to understand the motive, so that I can understand how far this thing goes. The King will not be satisfied with a badly done job." Will wipes his knife and slips it back into its scabbard.

"Then where do we go from here?" Rafe asks. "You say you know how the deed was done?"

"Yes. That is easy to demonstrate. The 'how' then reveals the 'who'," Will explains, "but I do not know why. Was it through anger, or a crime of gain? The motivation is important. I need to know some things, but I scarce know where to start."

"We have agents the length and breadth of the country, Will. Tell me what you need to know, and I will set our bloodhounds on the trail."

"Very well, Rafe," Will replies. "I need to know the entire history of someone, from the cradle to the present. There is a thread that runs through the killer's life, preparing him for this deed, and we must know it. Once we do, we will see who has been pulling the puppet's strings."

"Just give me a name."

"Patience, my friend. Moshe, will you find our master, and bid him arrange a meeting with the King for tomorrow, at nine? Tell him I wish him to *command* certain people to attend also. Here, I will write you a list." Moshe stands by, watching Will scratch down a number of names on a sheet of vellum. Then he rolls it up, and seals it with wax. The young man knows he cannot violate the seal, and smiles at his friend's quick wittedness. Will does not fully trust him yet. He thinks he will murder a full half of the court in revenge.

"I'll be off now," he says. "You will be able to reveal your killer's name to Rafe in perfect peace."

"Thank you, Mush, I knew you'd understand." Will hands over the scroll. "Take a slice of pie with you. You are an Englishman now, Master Morden."

"I fear the name will not stick, my friend. Besides, I prefer Mush ben Mordecai. It has a certain ring about it, don't you think?"

Rafe watches the young Jew leave, then turns to face Will Draper, who is writing a second note. A soldier who can write is an enigma, and he makes a mental note to keep on digging into Will Draper's misty past.

"Here, this is what I know of our killer. You have until nine tomorrow to find the thread I seek."

Rafe takes the note, and glances down at the name. He blinks, then looks up into his friend's eyes.

"You jest, surely?"

"No."

"Why would he wish to kill Isaac Ben Mordecai? It makes no sense at all."

"It does, if you look at events through a different set of eyes," Will says. "You must not think the obvious, my friend."

"I don't think anything," Rafe replies, grumpily. "I am, by my very nature, a man of the law. We deal in facts... even if we present them in a more beneficial way for our clients. It is nothing to do with either religion, or money, is it?"

"No. It is to do with secrecy... and time, Rafe. Find me what I need, and I will reveal all, tomorrow."

"And in the meantime?"

"I must visit a bawdy house near the Westminster dog pits," Will replies.

"Miriam will not be pleased." Rafe sniggers. Another funny story for the breakfast table is in the making. "Do not catch something evil before your wedding night."

"On the contrary, I hope I do," Will replies. "I wish to offer Harry Percy a personal invitation for the morrow. He is shut up safely in a whore house at the moment, and I must lure him out."

"And his part in all this?"

"I mean to reveal why he came to court so early, and why he brought Sir Drew Jennings along with him."

"Another riddle." Rafe is beset with doubts.

"One that Master Cromwell will be very interested in," Will Draper says. "I think I might enjoy tomorrow. It has the makings of a very interesting sort of day."

13   Norfolk's Gold

Will Draper's small room is lit by a single tallow candle, burning down to a splutter. It has a bed, a chair, and a table in it, and is the best York Place can manage at short notice for a mere Captain of the King's Horse. The other rooms are nicer, and filled with visiting nobles, ladies of the household, and the odd mistress or two. Those less fortunate are curled up on window sills, or asleep in chairs, or stretched, like dogs, outside barred doors.

He is almost asleep when his door opens an inch. He feels for the hilt of his dagger under the bolster, and closes his fingers about it. A short, dark shape slips into the room and stands, observing him. Will tightens his grip on the handle, and estimates the distance to cover. Two strides, and one thrust will do it, he thinks.

"I know you are awake," the voice says. "I'll wager you have a blade in your hand, even as I speak, by God's rattling teeth."

Will sits up slowly. The dark shape resolves itself into Thomas Howard, the Duke of Norfolk. He throws back the hood of his cloak, and crosses to the single chair.

"Do you mind? My legs are older than yours, Draper."

"Be my guest," Will replies, getting up to his feet. "I have nothing to offer you, my lord."

Norfolk produces a flask and bangs it down on the table. He has brought his own. Then he reaches into his doublet, and comes out with a heavy bag of coin. He rattles it, and places it alongside the flask of brandy.

"Fifty pounds," he says. "All yours, if you like."

"For what, my lord?"

"On the morrow, I am summoned to Henry's rooms for a meeting about this damned dead Jew banker. I want to know why. Do you intend charging me with his murder?"

"If you thought that, I would be dead already, sir," Will says, and the Duke laughs.

"True enough. I'd not baulk at killing even a Cromwell man, if my own life was under threat."

"It is, sir."

"What? You mean I am on the murderers list?" Norfolk is disquieted. He is no coward, but this killer can magic himself into rooms, and then disappear without a trace.

"I mean, if the killer succeeds in his aim, no one will be safe."

"Riddles," Norfolk says. "Tell me all you can."

"For fifty pounds?"

"A hundred then."

"Or a thousand."

"A thousand? Damn your thieving ways, you Irisher scum. I'll skin you alive!"

"Rest easy, sir." Will pushes the sack of gold back towards Norfolk. "I do not want your well intentioned bribe."

"What then?" Norfolk asks. "Everyone wants something. It is the way of things, and always shall be."

"Be less of an enemy to my master," Will Draper replies.

"Oh, I see Tom Cromwell's hand in this."

"No, sir. My master intends helping our sovereign lord, King Henry, in the great matter of his re-marriage, to your niece. Give him a little breathing space, I beg of you."

"Why should I?" The duke dislikes Cromwell for his low birth, but compared to him, everyone, bar Henry, is beneath the duke.

"Because he is the only man who

knows how to run England, now you have all killed Cardinal Wolsey," Will replies.

"The Duke of Suffolk said as much to me, the first time we met you," old Norfolk admits. "He says I do not know the price of wool!"

"The secret is to set the price, my lord, rather than know it," Will explains. "Thomas Cromwell is a good man, my Lord Norfolk. He knows the ways of business, and understands the law better than any other man in England."

Norfolk snorts, but sees the truth in what is said. He has a man to run his farms, and another to manage his ships. So, why not one to manage the country? God knows, he thinks, I don't want the bloody job!

"And what of the morrow?" he asks.

"Come armed. The king allows it, does he not?"

"He does."

"Then wear your sword, and have a few good men loitering about the place," Will Draper concludes.

"You expect trouble?"

"Perhaps. I don't know. It is late, my Lord Norfolk. May I return to my cold bed now?"

"At your age, my bed would have a

woman in it, making me warm," Norfolk growls.

"As will mine, once this affair is settled."

"I bid you good night then, Irishman." Norfolk is gone, as quietly as he arrived. On the table, the bag of gold lies unclaimed. Will shakes his head, unsure that he is not still dreaming the episode. He crosses to the door, opens it, and finds Richard and Rafe, stretched out, and fast asleep outside.

"Such fine watchdogs," Will mumbles to himself, and goes back to his cold bed.

*

"Do you know how much is in this purse?" Rafe Sadler asks.

"Fifty pounds." Will is busy making himself look as presentable as possible after his disturbed night.

"Where is it from?" Richard asks.

"The fairy queen came to me in the night, and paid it over, for favours rendered," Will says. "She likes handsome soldiers, you see."

"Really?" says Richard. Rafe takes off his cap and uses it to strike Richard about the head.

"Idiot. It's a bribe, but from whom?" he says. "No one got past us in the night."

"Really? Did you not hear Lord Norfolk ride up on his white maned charger, and batter down my door?"

Rafe Sadler is suitably chastened. He admits they might have dozed for a minute or two, and asks what the man wants of Will.

"To buy me," Will says, "but I think I struck a good deal for Master Cromwell instead. Norfolk might be a little friendlier towards him from now on."

"Nonsense." Richard Cromwell cannot believe his ears. "Even his own trained falcons are afraid to land on his wrist, for fear of him biting them. Norfolk is a ravening beast, who lives for nought but the comfort of Uncle Norfolk and his grand titles."

"Things change, Richard," Rafe tells him. "Perhaps Tom Howard wants our master to rid him of his wife too. After all, what is good for Henry, is good for England."

"Henry *is* England." Richard spreads his arms wide, to signify that his King is of the same size as his country, and grins.

"The house of Tudor will stand or fall, subject to him producing a male heir,"

Rafe says. Civil war is an ugly prospect, he thinks, and it must be avoided at any cost.

"The annulment is for Master Cromwell to handle. Did you find what I wanted?" Will is beginning to worry. It is no easy thing to confront a room full of lords and ladies, and conjure up a solution to an impossible murder.

"Of course. I have it here." Rafe produces a folded paper and passes it across. Will Draper opens it, and runs his eyes down a list of names. Most mean very little to him, and he grows despondent. It is when he reaches the last one there that his eyes light up.

"Are you sure of this alliance?" Will asks.

"Sure. It is through her first husband."

"And skilfully concealed," Will Draper says. "See how long this wicked thing has been planned, my friend? What infamy!"

"I agree," Rafe replies, "but I still do not know how Isaac ben Mordecai died."

"Come, let us collect Mush and Harry Cork on our way. What hour is it, Richard?"

"Not eight yet."

"Then we have time for breakfast." Will picks up the purse of gold and ties it to his belt. "A portion for Master Cromwell, and the rest amongst his young men."

"You learn quickly, Captain Will," Rafe says, smiling. "I wonder what Master Turner has cooking this morning?"

"Eggs, I hope. I can eat a dozen if boiled well," Richard tells them, seriously. Food is not a laughing matter to him. "Or perhaps some mutton cutlets, or jellied calves feet?"

They find Mush and Harry Cork chatting to two young women of the household. They have already eaten, so Will despatches them to loiter near the King's suite of rooms.

"Keep your eyes open, my friends, whilst Rafe, Richard and I go on a quest for boiled eggs."

*

"Ah, the ungodly pie thieves," the master cook says as they walk in to the kitchen. He crosses his hands over his immense stomach, and belches. "Come to do penance, my fine gentlemen?"

Will opens his purse, and drops a gold coin onto the table. The cook scoops it up, bites it and bows them to take a seat on one of the long benches. Unbidden, a small child appears, and lays out a series of platters, whilst another deposit's a loaf of hot bread, and a jug of weak beer in front of them.

"Any eggs?" Richard asks, hopefully. He has his strength to keep up, and the day promises to be a hard one. A few eggs will fit the bill nicely.

"Boiled, coddled, fried, poached, or scrambled in cream," the cook demands. He is an artist with eggs, often producing the most divine custards anyone has ever tasted.

"Boiled."

"Hard or soft? Never mind, you look like the hard boiled sort, with a little salt. I have some oak smoke cured ham if it pleases you, Master Will."

"Just some bread and cheese for me, Wat," Will replies. "How did our guest sleep?" The rotund cook smiles, as if he had just been given an entire sack of silver.

"He was a little fractious, at first, but two of my butcher boys hung him up in the meat store."

"Alive, I hope," Will says. "My Lord Percy is the guest of honour this morning. By special invitation. Has he been fed?"

"I tried, but the cold mutton proved

far too greasy for his stomach," Wat Turner tells them. "God alone knows what he's been supping, but he wretched until he was empty."

"I found him in a low bawdy house," Will explained to the company. "My young man, Adam Bright was keeping an eye on him, rather than on me." There is a sudden hush, and Rafe looks at Richard as if they are caught stealing apples. "It might amuse Master Cromwell to know the lad mistook him for a priest, and a notorious sodomite. I'm not angry with him, Rafe. Cromwell has watchers watching his watchers, and I see the sense of it."

"The boy failed in his duty," Rafe says. "He should have kept hidden from you."

"The boy chose his master," Will says. "What would you do, my friends, trust a black garbed sodomite priest, or me? I gave the lad a shilling, and told him to get along to Austin Friars."

"Hiring staff now, are we?"

"Rewarding loyalty," Will replies. "Adam Bright followed my orders to the letter, and did not fall asleep on the job!" There. That is the final word on it. Rafe and Richard failed to stay alert, and it might have been a killer, rather than Norfolk slipping past them in the night. They are suitably chastised, and can only hope the event does not become a comical tale told around Austin Friars breakfast table.

"I will have him taken on as a messenger," Rafe Sadler promises Will. "He can run notes between the house and the law courts."

"Excellent. I will see he learns his letters," Richard says, "and Will can teach him how to turn a blade, and administer a killing thrust."

"Eat your salted eggs, and mind you don't bite your tongue," Will tells him. "Ah, here is our guest. Good morrow to you, my dearest Lord Percy. Are you well?"

"You! You kidnapped me, and had me locked up with dead animals," Percy curses. "The King shall hear of this."

"Indeed he will, and within the hour, sir." Will places a document down in front of the Earl. It is a list of ingredients for making roast sucking pig with chestnuts, drawn up by Wat Turner. "Here, read this."

"I have a headache," Percy says, pushing it away. "Read it to me, if you think it important.

"It is a confession, sir," Will says,

coldly. "Written by Sir Andrew Jennings, in return for his life. He had a mind to visit France, suddenly."

"What?" Percy adopts a blank expression. "Drew Jennings has admitted to a crime?"

"At your order."

"He lies." The Earl looks from face to face, and sees that his word is not enough for Cromwell's men. "Bring him here, and I will say so, with my hand on the holy bible."

"You swear it was all his idea, alone, my Lord?" Will asks.

"I do. I knew nothing of it, until that morning." Percy is used to inferiors accepting his word. "Ask the man, if you ever find him."

Wat Turner sees Will nod to him, and swings open a store cupboard by the big hearth. Drew Jennings is trussed up inside, with his mouth gagged.

"Why, Sir Andrew, we thought you across the wide sea, in France by now," Will says to him. "His Lordship is outraged at your dastardly behaviour. What say you?" He tugs aside the gag.

"Bastard!" Jennings cries. "I told you to keep your stupid bloody mouth shut. See what you have done to us now? I will not let you take me for a fool, sir. For it was your wish. Yours alone." Will replaces the gag, and slams the door shut on him.

"Oh, dear. Perhaps we will let the King sort it all out," he says. "I think you might wish to think hard on what you say to him, Lord Percy."

"I do not recall ever speaking to Drew Jennings… about anything, you cur. That will suffice for my cousin Henry."

"The man who stole your wife?" Will says. Harry Percy makes a small choking sound in his throat, and his bloodshot eyes fill with tears.

"I spoke in jest," he says, weakly.

"In front of witnesses," Will Draper replies. "I might be a cur, Lord Percy, but I am Thomas Cromwell's cur. Which charge do you wish to face this morning? The crime you devised with Jennings, or the one that accuses you of marrying, then tupping the King's future wife… without permission of the crown?"

"Oh, dear Christ, but it is a lie." Percy is all false smiles. This is amongst friends, he wishes to say. Let us joke like red blooded men. "I spoke out in mere jest. As any of you might make a remark about any other man's wife. The King will not believe me capable of such a thing."

"Choose your guilt, Lord Percy," Will Draper says. Rafe and Richard are white faced with surprise. Will Draper has opened an old wound, and is using it, without compunction, to destroy the Duke of Northumberland right before their very eyes. "You might find the King more forgiving if you confess to the lesser crime. If he sees you abed with his lady, if only in his mind, he will have you broken, hanged, drawn and quartered for an *imagined* sin."

"Yes, it was imagined," Harry Percy says, grasping at the straw offered him. "We exchanged a poem or two, and I admired her from afar only. The entire kingdom knows her to be a chaste lady."

"Good. For if Henry spares you, Norfolk will not." Will pockets the fake confession. "He will ride north with a thousand troops, and use his canon to smash down your castle walls. He is not a forgiving man, My Lord Percy."

"What must I do?" Percy asks. He is a coward at heart, and looks to his own safety, first and foremost. If it means betraying friends, and denouncing lovers, then so be it.

"When I reveal your sin, you must

confess, then beg forgiveness," Will says. "That way, you will only be banished from court for a few months. Say Jennings was the real culprit, if you like. His life is forfeit anyway. I can do nothing to spare him from retribution."

"Yes, of course, it was all down to Drew Jennings," Harry Percy says. Give him a glass of wine and in a half hour, he will actually believe it to be so. "You, boy, I am thirsty. Bring me wine!"

Wat Turner steps forward, and cuffs the Duke casually behind the left ear. In this kitchen, he is king, and it is *his* will alone that shall be done. Harry Percy is not a brave bully. He takes the blow, whimpers, and slides down onto the rush strewn floor. The huge cook sighs, and beckons a boy across from his warm corner. He takes Percy by the collar, and hoists him, one handed, back onto the rough bench.

"Fetch this washed out wretch a flask of wine," he tells the serving boy. " The Italian rubbish, not the nice French red," he says.

"You are a true saint," Rafe Sadler sniggers to the master of all cooks. Wat Turner accepts the truth of this with a pious nod of his leonine head.

"A good morning's work, good sirs," he says.

"We are not yet done, Wat," Will says. "May we leave Drew Jennings in your custody for a few more hours?"

"Of course." The cook pauses, deep in thought. The question must be asked, he realises. "When all is settled, Master Will… I cannot have murder done in my kitchens. The king would be shocked at such a thing, and it might upset my routine. "

"Rest easy, sir. Some people will come and remove your prisoner," Will tells him. "His fate will be met well outside the walls of York Place."

"That will please the blessed soul of Cardinal Wolsey too," the cook replies. "Now, who will try these roasted cutlets?"

Richard Cromwell raises a single finger into the air. Boiled eggs and hot mutton cutlets will see him through the morning. Rafe and Will watch as he demolishes a platter of the steaming meat, and pick at their own food. Rafe pauses, with a piece of warm bread half way to his mouth.

"Do you believe this is the body of Christ, Will?"

"And that cold water can become good red wine?" Will Draper scowls. He remembers the priest demanding money before he would pray over his dead family. He still sees the dog's face in the night, now and then. "Wine into water is an easier trick. Does not Master Tyndale say that the change is not actual, but…"

"You've read Tyndale?" Rafe is surprised. It is forbidden, and the English bible can lead a man swiftly to the stake.

"Know thy enemy," Will says. "The king, Tyndale, Thomas More and Pope Clement all have their own views, and are each dangerous to us in different ways."

"Then what do you believe in?" Richard asks through a mouthful of meat.

"Master Cromwell, and my own sword arm." Will Draper stands, and brushes himself clear of any crumbs. "Ready, gentlemen?"

14   The Lair of the Winter King

Harry Cork and Mush are guarding the King's door, standing on each side, like wary dogs. Rafe thinks of Gog and Magog, the twin destroyers, prophesied for the Hebrew race, and smiles. Mush will soon be more English than Jew, and a convert to the faith that is Thomas Cromwell. He does not remember the old saying about beauty only running skin deep, and thinks the Jew beneath will not survive overlong.

There is still but one true God in Moshe ben Mordecai's mind, but he is content to serve an earthly master too. He will answer to Mush, and climb the slippery ladder with his new lord, and keep faith with the God of Israel too. Cromwell will call him a most pragmatic Jew, and love him for it.

"All present?" Will Draper asks. Rafe Sadler and the giant Richard Cromwell are flanking Harry Percy, who now looks fit for nothing but the shadow of the gallows. His face is haggard, and white with fear, and his legs are the elastic of the drunkard, and can scarcely support him.

"Everyone on the list, Will," Harry Cork tells him. "Though one or two are in a most black humour. I hope you know what you are doing, lest the king looks on you with disfavour."

"Rest easy, my friend," Will says. "Look here, and you will see that we have our man. Both of you, follow us in, close the door, and stand before it. None shall leave the chamber, save at the king's express orders. Is that clearly understood?"

Mush and young Harry Cork exchange glances. Will Draper is either struck suddenly mad, or he is the greatest fool in all of Christendom. Harry Percy is the Duke of Northumberland, defender of the Borders, and he is as close to the king as a blood brother. They usher the small party inside, and close the great wooden door. Inside the small room, all is silent.

Henry is seated in the best chair, behind the table. Norfolk is at his right hand, and the Duke of Suffolk is standing at the king's left shoulder. To one side, a little apart from these noblemen, is Thomas Cromwell, Sir Thomas More, his secretary Richard Rich, and the clergyman, Stephen Gardiner. By the corner screen, sitting on a well upholstered stool, is Lady Anne Boleyn, her pointed features composed into a mask of indifference. She is flanked by her brother George, the 2nd Viscount Rochford, and her sister, Lady Mary.

"Your congregation is assembled, Captain Draper," Thomas Cromwell says. "Though I am at a loss as to its ultimate purpose. Cannot you simply name the felon, and have the king give judgement?"

"Oh that it is so easy, Master Cromwell," Will Draper replies. "I must beg your indulgence, Your Majesty. All will be revealed to you in the fullness of time. Both guilt, and innocence must be shown, lest the blameless suffer in error."

"A fine point," Henry says and nods his head. "The law of England is there to protect, as well as punish my people. What say you, Thomas?"

"Never a truer word has ever been spoken, Your Royal Highness," Cromwell replies, but some true words are best unsaid, he thinks. The truth can start a roaring conflagration that even the River Thames cannot quench. He prays that Will understands the merit of truth, when taken in small doses. "Let the captain speak out. He is charged to act with independence, and even I know not what he will say to us."

Bravo, Master Cromwell, Will thinks. In one sentence he gives me leave to speak, and denies all blame if I step wrongly.

The next few minutes will be crucial, to all their futures. He takes a scroll from his tunic, and holds it up for all to see. Percy blanches with fear and makes a small mewing sound.

"You might have scraped your chin, cousin Percy," Henry says, as he notices Northumberland's condition for the first time. "You are not at a hunt now you know. Ladies are present!"

"My apologies, sire," Harry Percy mumbles, trying to make himself look as small as possible. "Circumstances forestalled me from tending to my usual toiletries."

"My fault entirely, Your Majesty," Will explains. "I rescued Lord Percy from a dangerous place, and locked him away safely, until just now."

"Hah!" Henry's expression grows cold. "You really must stop your carefree carousing, Percy. You are our strong right arm in the northern lands. Which makes me wonder why you are not there now."

"Let me answer that, sire." Will draws attention back to himself, and the tightly rolled scroll. "My master, Thomas Cromwell, recently had recourse to speak with Lord Percy, over a delicate matter of love. He did so at the request of Cardinal Wolsey, just before his sad death."

"Ah, was there ever a better servant to a king?" Henry casts down his eyes, and sighs. "I summoned him back, you know, Cromwell. It was my intention to forgive him."

Forgive his twenty years of loyal, devoted service, Thomas Cromwell thinks. Forgive his faultless running of England? He wants to tell this to his selfish king, but he cannot. Cardinal Wolsey, on his death bed, placed no blame on Henry.

"He told me so, sire," Cromwell says instead. "He had nothing but love in his heart for you, and was sure you would forgive him. You were, perhaps, misled by people who wanted him gone."

"Not dead though!" Norfolk cannot contain himself. "We all knew his worth, Henry. He just needed to be taken down a peg or two."

"Yes, he was a vain man, but a great servant," Thomas Cromwell says pertly. He sends Norfolk a look that says, 'shut up, before the king recalls your own heinous involvement'.

"Lord Percy took the cardinal's good advice, but formed a dislike for Master Cromwell. In his cups, he spoke ill of my master, rather as another, a king, once did about the sainted Beckett."

"Who will rid me of this turbulent priest," Henry mutters.

"But substitute the word 'lawyer' and you grasp my meaning, sire," Will tells the king. "A man close to the duke decided to fulfil Lord Percy's ill thought out wishes."

"Assassination!" Henry's blood runs cold. It is what he fears most. "You mean to tell me that Harry Percy sent someone to murder Tom Cromwell?"

Thomas Cromwell is all ears now. It is clear why Percy has come to court out of his usual season. He recalls marking him down in his black book once, and vows vengeance, no matter how long it takes him.

"Unwittingly, Your Majesty." There now, Will provides a way out for the king. "Once he realises the killer is on his way, he gives chase. He catches him, even as he reaches the court, and is in search of his victim."

"Infamous," Norfolk says, ambiguously. He is, as yet, unsure which way to let the wind take him. "So, Percy stops the man, you say?"

"He does, My Lord. The fool is locked up, and no harm done."

"No harm?" Henry is enraged. "One

of your louts comes to my court, intent on murder? Had he succeeded, I would have your head, Percy. Instead, you will return north. Find your dampest, coldest fortress, and shut yourself up in it, until I say otherwise. See to it Thomas. I will leave your would be assassin to your mercy."

Thomas Cromwell is short on mercy this morning. Harry Percy comes with a hardened killer, to slay him, and he is to be forgiving? He will strangle Drew Jennings with his own hands, and deal with his lordship later. He knows about Percy's boast against Lady Anne's virtue, and will use it to devastating effect, when the time comes.

"Hold hard," Norfolk says. "This is a pretty story, Draper, but it does not solve the murder committed in this very room. Come, my boy, tell us the truth. What of the dead Jew?"

"Patience, My Lord Norfolk." Will toys with the paper in his hand. "I must now touch upon why the Duke of Suffolk is present."

"Damned impudence," Henry says, and glowers at his erstwhile friend from childhood. "Charles Brandon is not in my favour any longer, sir. He is a … a… person of poor character."

"Not so, Your Majesty," Will tells the King. "He came to court to tell you how he is slandered. All the world knows of your deep love and friendship for the Duke of Suffolk, and some resent it."

"S t e a d y   o n ! "   N o r f o l k   i s uncomfortable. It is true that he dislikes Suffolk, who he considers to be a common upstart, but, in truth, he dislikes everyone who might detract from his own high position.

"I do not look to you, My Lord," Will says. "You have been a steady friend to all the king's best men. No, my investigation has brought up a significant fact. The young woman who claims to be Charles Brandon's lover is wrong. My men discovered that one of my Lord Suffolk's servants, assumed his identity to enhance his chances of bedding the lady."

"I don't believe it!" Henry is right not to, for it is a clever lie, but Will puts on as serious a face as he can manage. The foolish young man has confessed, and has been sent to work on Suffolk's estate in Ireland. The young woman, even after being disabused of her belief in the fellow's blue blood, has decided to go with him. Will explains all this with almost heart breaking candour, and leaves his audience almost speechless.

"All this tale needs for a happy ending, is for your friendship to be restored." Will Draper gestures for the two men to embrace, and they do. Henry is almost crying with relief. Brandon is a childhood friend, and that makes him special in the king's eyes.

"You forgive me, Harry?" Suffolk asks.

"There is nothing to forgive," Henry says, slapping his friend's back, heartily. "What a fine ruse though, Charles. Assuming a higher status to get a girl abed!"

"Alas, not one you can use, sire," Will says, and the King roars with laughter at the jest. Yes, who is higher than the king? He cannot look up, only down, so must rely on his natural charm to land a wench.

"You risked your life coming to my court," Henry says. He is becoming maudlin. "Did ever a King of England ever have so fine a friend?"

"It was not to clear his own name, sire," Will says. Wheels move within wheels, and Will Draper must play his hand out to the last card is down on the table. "He came, because he feared you might be listening to poor council."

"Is this so?"

"Er… yes," Suffolk says. He is lost now, but a happy thought comes to him. "Let young Draper explain. He speaks far more eloquently than I."

"Thank you, My Lord. It is clear that Suffolk and Norfolk are, together with my master Thomas Cromwell, the rocks upon which you build your kingdom."

"That is so," Henry says. "Cardinal Wolsey never failed to commend Cromwell to me. He has a fine lawyer's head, and a prince's good heart. That is how the Cardinal spoke of you, Thomas."

"God bless him," Will says. The rehabilitation of Cardinal Wolsey is almost complete. If the King can love Wolsey again, he can love Cromwell, as his chosen man. "It is of others that Suffolk wishes to speak, sire. He sees that powerful men in this realm still wish you to bend the knee to Pope Clement."

"What is this?" Sir Thomas More has been silent, but now, he is driven to say something. "A common soldier seeks to advise the King of England on religious matters? Is the world going mad before my very eyes, sire?"

"I speak only my Lord Suffolk's words, sir. He worries that there are people in court who are not fully behind the proposed marriage to the Lady Anne." Will turns, and bows to Anne, who is looking at More with daggers in her eyes. "He seeks only to warn you, sire."

"His thoughts are not dissimilar to mine," Henry says. "I understand your good intentions, Sir Thomas, and Master Gardiner's too, but you must understand the reality. My current marriage to Katherine is utterly false, and I *will* marry Lady Anne. On my oath!"

Thomas Cromwell is pleased. Will has learned his lessons well, and uses information as it is meant to be used. Percy, More and Gardiner are warned, and must scorn the King's wishes at their peril. Norfolk promises to show a kinder face to him, and Suffolk is made into a devoted friend. Well done. Is now the time to uncover the man who murdered Isaac ben Mordecai, he wonders?

"Then I must come to a very delicate matter, Your Majesty." Will twists the scroll between his hands. "A matter that might well cost me dear. May I speak frankly?"

"By God, you may," Henry says. He

is getting all his own way, and is ready to reward where it is due. "Speak without fear, young Draper. You have my word that you are safe."

"Very well. It touches the matter of Your Majesty's night time arrangements." Henry's face freezes into a mask of horror. He is caught. If he reneges on his promise, the whole court will know he has a secret to hide. "The court is a place where idle gossip is exchanged, and on each telling, it becomes ever more malicious."

Lady Anne and George glare at sister Mary, who smiles at Will, and nods her consent. He bows to her, and turns back to a horrified King of England who thinks his carnal secrets are to be laid bare for all to see, and laugh at.

"Even Sir Thomas More and Master Gardiner have heard the rumour that Lady Mary Boleyn visit's a lover, and that the man concerned is … you, Your Majesty."

"Preposterous!" It is all Henry can think of to say. He has his own peculiar set of morals, and finds it difficult to lie, even to save his own skin.

"Yes, it is." Will spreads his arms wide, as if offering himself up as a sacrifice. "For it is I who am to blame. Ever since I first saw Lady Mary at Esher House, I craved her love. I write her sonnets, and send little tokens of love. It is wrong, for I am to marry soon. My bride's brother is in this room, and I must beg his forgiveness."

Mush gives a small bow, if only to conceal the idiot smile on his face. Another tale for Cromwell's breakfast table is being born.

"It is true, my Lord," Lady Mary says. Will has primed her well, and promises lavish gifts for her co-operation. "I found the good Captain Draper to be a most comely man, and was much flattered. Then, I realised he was becoming far too infatuated with me, and put a stop to it."

"Yes, sire. She came to me on two occasions, and begged me to forget my desire for her. Regrettably, she was seen by idlers, and the rumour went about that it was you she visits."

"Absolutely preposterous!" Henry is back on safe ground. Lady Anne has been frowning too much of late, and was beginning to suspect another woman. "Still, I know what it is to love." He holds out a hand to Anne Boleyn, who smiles, and joins him.

"You are a remarkably brave young man to tell us this, Captain Draper," she says. "My sister is a Boleyn, and therefore has a certain attraction to men. Many men have felt as you do, I suppose... though I do not see it myself... but it will pass, will it not, my love?"

"Oh, yes." Henry nods his head with vigour, and relief. "I forgive you, of course, but you must not aim above your station, Captain Draper!" Will Draper bows, and sighs, as if his heart is about to break asunder. There, the king is saved from Lady Anne's jealous wrath.

"You are too gracious, sire... Lady Anne," Will says.

"I will keep the lad busy, your majesty," Thomas Cromwell says to the regal couple. "Between work and his new bride, he will have no time for this courtly love."

George Boleyn leans and whispers in his sister Mary's ear. In less than brotherly terms he sneers at her bad taste in men. She has soiled the family name, or so he thinks, with her misplaced lustfulness. Mary gives him a cursive look, and mutters back a certain name. George is startled at what she knows, so moves away to lick his wounds. It is bad enough to be kicked by Anne, without Mary having the whip hand over him.

"I believe we should have a scribe summoned, sire," Norfolk says. "For all these tales rival the stories we can read about the fabled King Arthur and his court."

"I think not, Norfolk," Suffolk says to him. "For few of us are shown in an altogether goodly light."

"God's flaming tongue, Brandon," Norfolk replies. "I am growing old, listening to one clever story after another. You are a saint, come to rescue Henry from his wicked counsellors. More and Gardiner are serpents, and Thomas Cromwell is able to walk on water, and part the Red Sea!"

"What is that you say, Uncle Norfolk?" The King has stopped paying loving attention to La Boleyn, and hears the tail of the Duke's sharp comment. "Who is it who walks on water?"

"Captain Draper, it would seem," Cromwell says, diverting the King from a scowling Norfolk. "He is reminding us of friendship, and our duty to God and the king. My Lord Suffolk is reconciled to you, by his doing, and you see clearly where each man's loyalties lie. I think we might say this is a good morning all around."

"You speak for us all," Stephen Gardiner says, rather stiffly. "For we all want that which His Majesty desires, whilst still allowing His Holiness to save face. Pope Clement's concern is to keep the legitimate church from harms way."

"The *legitimate* church, you say? Spoken like a true lawyer, Stephen," Thomas Cromwell says. Legitimacy is a touchy subject with Henry, and one Gardiner should avoid. "You know well enough that Pope Clement can always save face... for it is said that he has two of them."

"Have a care," Sir Thomas More mutters. Kings may come and go, but the church is everlasting, and it has a long memory. The Lord Chancellor knows that if Henry dies, powerful men will fight to put Princess Mary on the throne. Then, Master Cromwell, he thinks, we will see who has two faces!

"Do not misunderstand me," Cromwell replies, loud enough for the King to stop stroking the Boleyn arm. "I believe the Pope must be brought to understand King Henry's needs, and smooth the path to the correct conclusion. It will take a rare man to bring him around from his current way of thinking."

"A rare man, Thomas?" the king asks.

"Yes, Your Highness. I think Master Gardiner will do a fine job for us. He is an ordained cleric himself, and can argue the finer points of canon law. Who better to sway the papacy than he?"

"By God, yes, Thomas. You are right." Henry is very pleased with the idea. "See to it for us."

"At once, Your Majesty." Thomas Cromwell says. Gardiner almost faints with shock. Italy is awash with fever, outlaws and rampant mercenaries. Cromwell is ecstatic. Stephen Gardiner is a constant thorn in his side. His removal to Rome for six months, or even a year, will work wonders for the peace of the court.

He will never manage to change Pope Clement's venal mind, of course. Not without a huge bribe. Rome will stand on its usual moral high ground, Henry will be furious, and Thomas Cromwell's great scheme for the reordering of England will progress without further hindrance.

Richard Rich, who has remained silent and invisible until now, steps forward, and pats Stephen Gardiner on the back. He mutters a few, reassuring words, and promises to keep an eye on his law caseload. The lawyer glares at his friend, knowing that he will also keep an eye on his sisterly mistresses. Cromwell is pleased, as Rich is a man who is easily bought, and will serve Henry's cause well, in return for a knighthood, or a few acres of good land in the depths of Kent, or Worcestershire.

"Ah, my dear old Gardiner," the Duke of Norfolk cackles, "do give my fondest regards to your pox ridden Pope Clement. Now, for the last time, Will Draper... who, in Hell's blasted name murdered the king's Jew banker?"

15   Revelations

Will Draper thinks he is in danger of losing his audience. Perhaps he has made too many revelations, and told one clever tale too many? He can only admire the way Master Cromwell has taken advantage of a half chance to rid himself of the troublesome Stephen Gardiner for six months, but it is time to bring the entire affair to a head.

"Your Majesty, my Lords, and Ladies, pray attend my words carefully." The room quietens again. There, that is a much better atmosphere in which to conduct a piece of magic. "In a moment or two, a man will knock on the door, and crave entry. Admit him, Mush, for he knows who the killer is, and how he did the foul deed."

Every eye turns towards the door. You can hear them breathing, some calm, and some laboured of breath. Henry thinks something wondrous is about to happen… something quite magical, and he shivers at the prospect. Mush and Harry Cork move from the door, and turn to face it, with hands on dagger hilts. Seconds pass, and the quiet becomes unbearable. Then, quite distinctly there is the sound of three sharp raps on the outer door.

Even though it is clearly foretold to them by Will Draper, the women gasp, and shudder in superstitious fear. Harry Cork stands and stares open mouthed, but young Mush ben Mordecai is made of far sterner stuff. He steps forward, unlatches the door, and swings it wide open. Captain Will Draper steps into the room, and everyone gasps in astonishment.

"What is this?" Norfolk looks to his left, where a moment before Draper had stood, talking to them. "Is this some damned witchery, Master Draper? Shall we pile the faggots high, and burn you for it?"

"For a simple trick?" Will pushes through the gathering, and stops in front of the king. "I see you thinking, sire. Speak your thoughts out loud, for lesser mortals to understand."

"A secret passage of some sort," Henry pronounces, and they all say 'of course', and 'how clever of Henry to know the trick'. In truth, Thomas Cromwell has muttered the secret into the king's ear, even as the door is opened. By nightfall, Henry will believe he guessed all by his own self, and that he is the cleverest monarch in all Christendom.

"Built by Cardinal Wolsey's

builders," Will explains. "This room was his bedroom, and the room next door was for his special guest. I am told she was a pleasant looking lady, though not of the highest birth."

"I knew it!" Norfolk is almost choking with laughter. "Old Wolsey had a mistress. The cunning fox outwitted us all there."

"She would slip from room to room by means of a secret door, set in the panelling and cleverly concealed behind the screen," Will says.

"How do you know this?" Henry demands. He is a prudish man in the matter of other men's morals, and he is shocked at his old cardinal's worldly lustfulness.

"There was a clue, sire. On that first morning, I noticed the candle on the clock was out. Yet you say it was lit well enough when you left the room."

"It was. The Jew, Isaac, was sitting in front of the screen, and the candle was lit." The king is curious now. He knows magic is not involved, so wants some answers. "I had to light the lamp nearest the table too."

"You closed the door, and the secret panel was opened but a moment later. The draft thus caused blew out the candles. The murderer slipped in, into the darkened room, perceived someone sitting in your chair, and stabbed them from behind. Then they slipped out, closing the secret panel behind themselves."

"I do not understand how that could possibly be," Henry says to Will. "My early morning meeting was a secret. How did they know Isaac was with me?"

"They did not, sire," Will tells him, and watches the look of horror cross the king's face as he realises the truth. "They came with but one intent in their heart. To murder the King of England."

"Assassination!" Norfolk takes a step closer to Henry. "To think, how close they came to it."

"The candle blowing out was a clue," Will continues, "but it took a while for me to see the significance. Once I suspected a secret way in, I went to one of the oldest servants here in York Place, and questioned him about when the place was first built. Back then, Wat Turner was cook to Cardinal Wolsey, and knew the old secret."

"Then the cook must have told the assassin about it," Lady Anne says. She is shivering with fear, for if Henry falls, so to does the entire Boleyn family. "Have him arrested at once, Henry. He must be put to the question!"

"Not so, my lady." Will gestures to the intricately carved wooden screen. "This particular secret was told, in all innocence, by another, many years since. They mentioned it in the hearing of a small child and, in later times, the wicked plot was conceived, using that knowledge. A secret way to the king had been uncovered, and by those who bear him the greatest ill will of all."

Will Draper uses his master's teachings well. In one sentence, he has reminded Henry that it is he who is to be thanked, that the plot was wicked beyond forgiveness, and that there are those, despite the king's high opinion of himself, who want him dead.

"Then the poor Jew was killed by accident?" The Duke of Suffolk is a little slower than the rest, but finally understands what has happened.

"The candle was out," Will Draper reiterates. "The killer made a rather simple mistake in the dark. I can only imagine that he was so frightened of what he must do that he failed to make a proper identification of his victim." Mush hisses, and curses under his breath. That his grandfather has died without good reason seems to make the crime all the worse in his eyes.

"You know who it is, Captain Draper?" Henry has backed himself up against the panelled wall of the room. He sees himself as suddenly beset by would be assassins. The Duke of Norfolk frowns at Draper's cleverness, and rests his hand on the dagger concealed within his blouse.

"Of course. It is obvious, once you remember the rose petals floating on the water." Will takes the time to look each person directly in the eye. He sees the returning look of fear from one, and knows that he is right for sure. "Behind each screen, there is a small table, or pedestal,   with a bowl of rose petal strewn water set upon it. It is placed fresh, each morning, in all the royal chambers. The killer, if he were some outside agent, would not know this small fact, and coming through the secret door, would knock it over... seeing as how he would be in the dark."

"Oh, I see," Thomas Cromwell says as he sees now who the murderer must be. "How *very* clever."

"Only someone used to this arrangement would know enough to step around the roses in the gloom."

"Then who is it?" Henry is white faced, and wants only to be told. The moment is upon them, Will perceives.

"Only a trusted household servant would know," he says. "Isn't that right, Master Cork?"

Harry Cork's face betrays his guilt. He has failed once to rid England of a tyrant, and now, must take his last chance. A quick dash forward, sword drawn, and thrust it deep into Henry's bloated body, he thinks. His hand is barely on the hilt of his sword before Mush transfixes him with an upward dagger thrust into the heart. Between the ribs, Will Draper has explained, and twist it to rip open the heart. Death, he is assured, is almost instantaneous.

He takes the weight, and lowers the body to the floor. A woman screams. It is not Anne: she is fearless. George Boleyn has drawn a dagger, as have both Norfolk and Suffolk. The room bristles like a porcupine with steel quills. Will raises his hands, and gestures for the deadly blades to be hidden away.

"My good Lords, remember where you are," he says. "It is an offence to bring concealed weapons into the King's presence.

There, another point for Cromwell's side. Will reminds Henry Tudor that his security is poor, and should be looked at by far more competent men than he currently employs. Men like Tom Cromwell's young fellows. "Though I am sure his majesty will forgive you, because of your honourable intentions. They seek only to save Your Highness, sire."

"It is forgiven," Henry murmurs. For a moment, he feels like Caesar standing at the foot of Pompeii's statue, and he shudders. "Pray, Master Cromwell, have your gentlemen remove the assassin's corpse. It is disturbing the ladies."

Harry Cork is dragged from the room. Will crosses himself as the sightless eyes fall on him. It is better this way, Will thinks. Had you been taken, Harry Cork, your death would have been prolonged, and indescribably painful. In France, your arms and legs would be tied to four horses, and here, your entrails would be plucked from you, even as you breathed your last.

*

The room is silent. No one quite knows what to say or do. The King, thank God, is still alive, but what of the next assassin? If Henry dies, they think, the country will erupt into a bloody civil war.

None knows this better than Thomas Cromwell. The northern shires will demand Princess Mary takes the throne, and the Howard clan, led by Norfolk will oppose them. Suffolk, for now, will side with Norfolk.

Henry Fitzroy, the bastard son of Henry and Bessie Blount is at the age of ten, still too young, but there are some, like the Welsh aristocracy, who would wish him to ascend the throne. Then there are the old royalty. There are living Plantagenet's, like the Pole family who Henry should have had killed years ago. They will wish to sweep the Tudor dynasty aside, and restore the old order.

Politics within politics, Thomas Cromwell thinks, and which ever party wins, they will want his head on a spike! He pushes between Norfolk and the King, whispers in his ear, then raises Henry's hand to his lips.

"Almighty God, and *my* man Captain Will Draper, has preserved you life today, sire," he says. "Now, there are urgent steps to take. Send them all away, save for Draper." Henry nods, once. In all of this, it has been Cromwell, or Cromwell's man who has stood between he, and a violent death.

"Leave us," he says. "Captain Draper, you will stay. My lady, back to Esher with you. Norfolk, Suffolk… I never doubted you for a moment. You are ever in my thoughts. I thank you for your devotion to my person. Keep close, Charles… as a friend, rather than a counsellor."

The two Dukes breath easier. In such circumstances, it is easy for a King to throw the baby out with the bath water, and Dukes heads have adorned the gates of London before. They both remember the Duke of Buckingham, condemned merely for listening to a prophesy of the King's future death.

Henry waits until the room is emptied, then allows himself to slump down into his chair. There is a sudden banging from the next room, and he starts like a scared rabbit.

"Be calm, sire," Will Draper says. "I gave orders for the court carpenters to seal the secret door up. I did not realise they would be so attentive to their duty."

"Well thought of, young fellow," Henry says, regaining his regal aspect. He is reminded how this commoner has saved his and Lady Mary Boleyn's honour. "You are a good servant to your master."

"I serve Master Cromwell, sire, but you are master of us both," Will tells him. Over and over, Cromwell has said, the King must be reminded of our worth. If he seeks advice, let it be from Thomas Cromwell, or one of his household. If he seeks a confidant, let it be one of us. "I take my instruction from Master Thomas, he obeys you, and you listen to what God puts into your heart."

The carefully learned phrase has now been planted in Henry's mind. Cromwell is beginning the steady move away from Roman Catholic Rome. The king is subject to none, save God.

"Then I tell you this, God has put it into my heart to reward you, Master Cromwell. Choose whatever you will, and I shall bestow it upon you. I leave it to you to pass a portion of your new acquisition to your young fellows, for they have served us both most well."

"Your Majesty is too kind," Cromwell says, but he already has his list of gifts, and will suggest one in due course. "Though I must ask you to attend to a more pressing matter first. Captain Draper saved your life today, but what of tomorrow?"

"Tomorrow?"

"Harry Cork did not act alone,"

Thomas Cromwell explains. "He is but the instrument of other, more dangerous people. Speak, Will. The King wishes to hear the full story, so that he may decide where the true guilt lies, and what punishment must be meted out to these would be regicides."

Regicide: to kill a king. The word alone is enough to make Henry tremble with horror. He is the chosen one. The people of England, the aristocracy, and the church accept him as the one, anointed with sacred oil, to rule this great realm. He beckons Will Draper forward.

"You have my ear, young man," Henry Tudor says. "Tell me the whole sorry tale."

Will bows, and starts his report with a sin. He explains how, whilst travelling the realm, from diocese to diocese, Cardinal Thomas Wolsey was wont to break his vow of chastity. It is a tale heard from the old cook, who, like most long serving men, kept his ears open.

"The Cardinal always considered his vow to be one made more in the spirit of the thing," Thomas Cromwell mutters. "In all other respects, he was a good churchman, and a loyal subject, sire." Henry nods at this pragmatic explanation. He understands that every man has carnal needs, even popes, and that such needs are often filled against the hidebound strictures of the church.

Will continues. He mentions several places stopped at, and several women taken to the amorous cardinal's bed. They last only for a night or two. Then, he sees a woman of quite low birth, who has become a much sought after seamstress, and attempts a seduction. He is quite firmly rebuffed. Not to be beaten, he renews his courtship by finding her a position in one of the grander houses.

"We should skip over the various stages of seduction, Your Majesty," Will Draper says. "It would be prurient to dwell on the great Wolsey's tactics."

"Of course," Henry agrees.

"Suffice to say, the Cardinal finally reaps his reward," the soldier continues. "The woman is brought to York Place from time to time, and Wolsey has the secret panel fitted, to facilitate ease of access. In those days, this room was Wolsey's master bedroom. It can tell a tale or two, if only the walls could talk." The King smiles, pleased that they cannot speak of his own indiscretions, and urges Will on to finish his story.

Will Draper tells of how Wolsey

keeps the woman as his mistress for two whole years, before tiring of her. He is a good man though, and cannot simply cast her out into the cold world. She has an older sister, and a brother-in-law, who live over in Worcestershire. He bestows a farm house, some livestock, and a hundred acres of fine land on the woman, stipulating that the hard working brother-in-law and his sensible wife move in, and run it for her.

She is content, and spends her time making dresses for the local gentry. It brings in enough, when the farm profit is added, to provide a decent standard of living. They sit about the fire of an evening, and she tells tales of how she was once the mistress of the highest cleric in the land. It is amongst family, so not considered indiscreet. This much, Will has had from Henry's old cook.

"Now, comes the twist of fate," Will Draper tells the king, who is leaning forward in rapt attention. Rafe Sadler's spies have found out what happened then. "The older sister already has a child… a small boy, who absorbs every word he hears. The boy's name is Harry Cork. He grows up, and goes to seek his way in the world. By the greatest mischance, he is taken on at one of the great houses his aunt used to work for."

"Mischance you say?" Henry puts in.

"Yes, sire… for Harry Cork is a boastful young man, and talks of his aunt, her time spent at York Place, and of her affair with Cardinal Wolsey. The mistress of the house gets to hear about these tales, and she sends for him. She forms an attachment … a rather *sentimental* attachment… to the lad. She is rather too fond of younger men."

"Lady Hurstmantle," Thomas Cromwell says, softly. It is best coming from him. The damnable woman is a distant relative of the king, on her first husband's side. Though she is related to the Plantagenet bloodline too. The King sighs heavily.

"Is nothing in this life easy," he curses. "The damned woman should learn to keep herself out of my business." This said, he bids Will Draper finish his tale.

Will is on firm ground now. He can tell the tale from first hand knowledge, rather than the gossip picked up from servants.

Harry Cork is smitten by the older woman's physical charms, and soon becomes a loyal follower of her doctrine. Lady Jane Hurstmantle is a devoted friend to Queen Katherine, and utterly opposes the King's will in the matter of the annulment.

The reasoning is flawed, but it appeals to her sense of self righteousness. If only Anne Boleyn were out of the way. King Henry might see the error of his ways, and reconcile himself to Katherine and Pope Clement. Then Princess Mary would rule afterwards, keeping England firmly in the true faith. The followers of Luther, and the readers of Tyndale will go to the stake, and England will be saved. This is how she plays on her followers minds, and bends them to her way of things.

"The wicked old bitch!" Henry cannot contain himself. The depth of the betrayal has stricken at his heart. "To even *think* of the king's death is high treason," he cries.

"Not in English law," Thomas Cromwell says, "but it can be, Your Highness. Given authority, and a little time … it can be."

"Lady Jane Hurstmantle thinks to meddle in the king's affairs, and she has a half baked plan," says Will Draper. "She has heard of a certain Flemish alchemist who can seemingly kill with dolls, and so, she seeks him out. I was able to thwart her plan, and visit swift retribution on her foreign poisoner."

"For which I am grateful, young man," Henry interposes.

"Harry Cork has a much grander idea though. Why not put little Princess Mary on the throne at once?" Will continues. "All that needs to be done, is effect the immediate death of Henry. Her ladyship, we must assume from her continued support of him, is taken with the idea. If they could only get close to the king. Close enough to deliver a decisive killing blow."

"Then you believe the woman is as guilty as the assassin?" the Duke of Suffolk asks. He has been standing quietly to one side, but can hold his tongue no longer. "You think her to be the true instigator?"

"I do, sir. Harry Cork has been played like a fish on a line. He thinks it is all his own idea to volunteer. He will find a way to get into Henry's court, and wait for a chance." Will pauses, and glances at those around the king. "It is about then that certain people conspire to have His Majesty issue an arrest warrant for Cardinal Wolsey."

"A bad day's work," Henry says. "I meant only to reprimand him in private conversation. Why was I so swayed?"

"You were persuaded by clever men, with their own idea of how you should run your country, sire." Cromwell says. He will continue the process, until Henry is convinced he was tricked into Cardinal Wolsey's downfall. Then Norfolk, Suffolk and Harry Percy will dance to an altogether different tune. The words are Cromwell's, and Will is but the winged messenger.

"Cork attached himself to Lord Percy's retinue, and managed to join the arrest party," Will explains to them. "Which is where he came across me. He was friendly, and he gave me some very good advice. In return, I recommended him to Master Cromwell. To give him his due, my master did not take to the fellow at all. He would not employ him inside Austin Friars."

"It was only that he was not the sort of lad I could use," Thomas Cromwell tells them. "He would be fine at fetching and carrying, but of no use for anything that required wits. So, I, like a damnable old fool, set him working in York Place. It was the single worst mistake I have ever made, sire."

"I do not blame you, Thomas," Henry says. "You sought only to put good young fellows around me. Why, I even pressed you to do so, did I not, my friend?"

"He was very keen to please," Will says. "According to your household stewards, he rushed to do any small service, and eventually asked if he might put in place the rose petal water bowls each morning. For he longed to glimpse the king. Such devotion, they think, and so they let him take on the small, onerous job. No one realises that he has another motive. It is his moment. He is placed exactly where he wants to be."

"So close," Henry says.

"Yes, sire. If you had not taken Isaac ben Mordecai into your room, you might well have died that day. Harry Cork was waiting, next door. His plan was simple enough. Each morning, he would linger at his task... hoping to be there at just the moment you are alone in one of the two royal chambers. After weeks of frustration, his luck seems to change for the better. He hears the noises in this chamber... your own private room... and he decides to strike. He slips in, avoiding the water bowl deftly, and finds the room in darkness. Opening the secret door has caused a sudden draft, and the clock candle is blown out. Never mind, he thinks, the layout of the chamber is familiar to him, even in the dark. He steps out from behind the screen, and makes out a dim shape, seated in Henry's chair. Who else can it be, but the king? He draws his dagger, leans over his victim, and strikes into the heart."

"The fiend!" Henry feels queasy, and clutches at his own heart, as if it is pierced by proxy. "That so young a fellow could be so callow."

"It was that which first led me to suspect," Will Draper says, though now he is boasting. It is only later that he realises the import of something the young man had said to him. "When I first spoke with Harry Cork, he knew the victim had been stabbed in the heart. How could he know such a detail, unless he was the assassin?"

16   A King's Forgiveness

"Steady on there, Mush!" Richard Cromwell says to his eager young companion. "I can scarcely keep apace of you, my lad. Slow down, for there is no mad rush." They are pushing a wooden, two wheeled handcart, borrowed from York Place's sprawling kitchens. For the purpose of transporting some meat, Mush tells the cook, Wat Turner. This particular meat is freshly killed though, and destined for the swirling waters of the Thames. In a few days, Harry Cork's mortal remains will wash out into the vast anonymity of the English Channel.

"I looked into his eyes as I struck," the younger man says. "He knew it was I who took his life. My grandfather would be proud of me, and the way I avenged his wickedly done death."

"Perhaps," Richard replies. "Here, the river is fast at this point. The body will be out at sea by nightfall. May God curse his stinking soul." There is a loud splash, but no one bothers to turn and look. Best not to know, or show any curiosity. The two young men are wearing Cromwell livery, and that is enough to deter anyone's curiosity.

London is learning fast. It is not wise to cross a Cromwell man.

*

"Well, Drew Jennings, you look a sorry sight." Rafe sees the half healed scars where dogs have bitten, and the bruises from the beating he received when being stuffed in his captive cupboard. "You know me, sir?"

"I do," Jennings says. He recognises the Cromwell dress, and the close shaven red hair that covers a large skull. "Are you here to kill me then?"

"What do you take us for?" Rafe replies. "We are not Spaniards, or even French. Master Cromwell decrees that the punishment must fit the crime. You sought to murder my master at the behest of yours. No, do not dare try to deny it, you cur. All is known. Lord Harry Percy wept like a newborn baby, and swore it was all your own doing. Your plan, from start to finish."

"That dirty bastard," Drew Jennings says. "I am but the mirror of you, Master Sadler. I reflect only what my master wishes. If he bids me kill… what else can I do?"

"Well enough spoken." Rafe sits on the edge of one of the big tables, and toys with a wooden ladle. "You are disowned by the Duke of Northumberland, and therefore without a master. Thomas Cromwell bids me offer you two courses. The first is to give you a day's start. Run as fast as you can, and hide away. If you are then caught, my master reserves the right to take your life from you."

"A very fair offer," Drew Jennings replies. "And the second?"

"Swear yourself to him," Rafe says.

"Every pack has its leader," Drew Jennings mutters. "One dog is much as another. I will serve your Cromwell, if he so wishes."

"He does." Rafe considers for a moment. "He is a harder taskmaster than Lord Percy, but he is a fairer man."

"Then I am his man," Jennings confirms. "It is better than having to run away, and hide."

"What then if he asks you to do something … terrible?" Rafe asks.

"There is nothing I have not done… and nothing I would not do," Jennings boasts. "Pay me enough, and I would slit God's own throat, and smile at the thought of it."

"You are so able?" Rafe asks the man, but he knows the answer.

"Try me."

"Very well then … here is your new master's first instruction to you."

*

"Does this roasted chicken taste well enough to you, my dear Cromwell?"

"Or is it *fowl*, sire?" Thomas Cromwell smiles at his little jest, and bites into a drumstick. "It is perfect. I will send you my very own poultry cook. He has a way of basting a bird that makes the mouth water with pleasure."

Henry fears every dish is now poisoned, but is somewhat reassured when Cromwell calls for Wat Turner to come up from the kitchens. The huge cook explains, in detail, every step in preparing food for the king. Everything is fresh. It is locked away until needed, then tasted during, and after, the cooking process.

"Then, Your Majesty," Wat declares. "I taste it myself. Finally, the dishes are presented in a random order. No man, waiting on, can know which platter will end up in front of the King. Even then, the man who stands behind you tastes each dish before it is set down."

"Stout fellow," Henry says, then laughs. He has made a lame jest, so the rest of the court must laugh too. Wat Turner, pleased to have finally met King Henry, slaps his hand on his belly. The noise resounds throughout the banquet hall to gales of applause.

"I've been eating my own food for the best part of thirty five years, sire," he says. "The Cardinal, God bless him, ate it for upwards of twenty. It has done me no harm, and poor Wolsey neither."

"There was never a better man to know, Master Turner." Henry has convinced himself of this, and Norfolk tries to keep out of the king's line of sight. "I see you shrink away, Tom Howard. You do well to, for you and your like hounded the poor man to his untimely grave."

"May we discuss the matter of treason, Your Majesty?" Cromwell has a list, and wishes to put names in to Henry's mind for future consideration. "Your idea about making the thought alone treasonable has its merits… but also its pitfalls. May me speak of it more?"

"If we must." Henry dislikes unpleasantness, but sees it must be faced up to. "Lady Jane Hurstmantle has behaved in a ridiculous, even treasonable, way. It is always so when such flighty women try to think. What shall we do with the poor demented creature, sir?"

Thomas Cromwell thinks a sharp axe will suffice, but there is a serious problem to overcome. Apart from being a woman, Lady Jane was at the court when Henry's father died. She consoled Henry for a few months, and is still fondly remembered as an accomplished lover, in the French way. So he treads carefully, and councils clemency.

"Had it been a man, no matter who, I would say… death. The lady is, as you perceive, somewhat muddled in her mind. It must be to do with her inflamed sexual desires. Perhaps a stiff letter from Your Highness will suffice to cool her ardour for your death. You might suggest she visit her cousin in Durham for a year or two."

"Her cousin?" Henry prides himself on knowing the bloodline of all those aligned to the Tudor house, but he is at a loss to know whom is meant.

"Several times over removed, but still an actual blood relation to her, I am told." Cromwell almost smiles at the delicious revenge he is taking. "Harry Percy's heralds will know better what the exact relationship is."

"Percy? By God, Cromwell…. Do

you think he…?"

"There is no proof of a political connexion, sire," Tom Cromwell says, "but my people will look into it, most carefully. My Lord Percy has irked you several times of late."

"He has."

"Might I suggest you sequester one of his castles, and hand it over to My Lord Suffolk?"

"To Charles?"

"Why not? It will cement your friendship." And bind Suffolk to me all the tighter, he thinks. "I have other names on my list. All men."

"Are they proven to be traitorous?" Henry loves the law, but he loves his own safety far more.

"Beyond doubt, sire." Cromwell grimaces. "They defame you most wantonly in the matter of the divorce, and support the Plantagenet cause."

"Are any of them of the aristocracy?" the king asks, warily. It does not do to lop off the heads of too many powerful men, in case it gives the rest rebellious thoughts.

"No, Your Majesty. One mayor, still stubbornly loyal to Katherine, a couple of Thomas More's more outspoken friends, and

Stephen Gardiner's ex secretary. You did mention the penalty for men, I believe?"

"Do it." Henry waves his hand, as if granting permission. It will keep More and Gardiner honest, if nothing else."

"It will be done, sire," Cromwell says. The men are all enemies of either himself, or the late cardinal, and thus a danger to all.

He must also compose a stiff letter to Lady Jane Hurstmantle, who is to be spared because she once gave Henry a delightful lesson in the *French* way of things. It is, he thinks, only for show and, if his plan goes well, will not need to be delivered.

*

"Is it done?" Miriam is sitting in front of a mirror. It is Flemish made, and cost Cromwell the equivalent of a small house. He has one in every bedroom. Will nods. He tells her only that Harry Cork is the man, and that Mush has settled the matter honourably.

"Your grandfather's soul can rest now," Will says.

"We do not have souls," Miriam says. "We are Jews, and not allowed them. Mush and I will play out our roles in public, but in private, we are true to our God."

"You can worship a buttered parsnip, for all I care," Will Draper replies. "Just as long as you marry me, my girl."

"Don't mock religion so freely, my dearest one," Miriam says. "I think that a storm is coming. Soon now, men will kill over which language your holy book is to be written in. Through no fault of our own, we find ourselves allied to but one faction, and our enemies will multiply with each passing day.We will be like the lost tribe of Israel, and all men's hands will be against us."

Will understands, but he is beginning to feel the sense of invincibility that all of Tom Cromwell's young men acquire. He has saved the king from assassination, and radically advanced the Cromwell cause. Power and riches are there for the taking, if only he holds his nerve, and keeps faith with Thomas Cromwell.

"Let your mind rest easy, Miriam," he says. "Under this roof, we have nought but friends. Come with me now, for the priest is waiting."

"Moshe wishes to give me away, because he is my only living blood," she tells him, "but he thinks your Master Cromwell might wish to reserve that honour to himself. After all, I am living under his roof… and he is the master here."

"He does not seek to replace your grandfather, or Mush," Will says. "He is content to watch events from the side. It is what he does so well."

"You think Master Thomas is a benign observer then?" Miriam asks. Will smiles then.

"Sometimes," he replies.

*

Sir Andrew Jennings stands for a moment, and allows his eyes to become accustomed to the dim light. There are but a brace of candles in the luxurious bed chamber. The great house is draped in silence, and even the hounds in their kennels are asleep at this hour.

It is a small matter for Drew Jennings to scale the wall, ease open the shutter, and slip through the gap, and into the sleeping chamber. He crosses to the bed in three cautious strides, and sees that there are two bodies slumbering therein. One, a woman, is lying on one side, and she is both buxom, and naked. The other is a man. He is lying on his back, slack of jaw, and snoring softly.

The intrusive noise stops as Sir drew Jennings slides a keen edged knife across his throat. There is a spray of blood, the young man's muscular body jerks once, and then is still. Jennings glides around to the far side of the huge bed, and touches a finger to the woman's naked shoulder.

She stirs then, blinks her eyes, and turns over. She sees the dead man beside her, and is about to scream, but the calm assassin is on her at once. He clamps a strong hand about her white throat, and squeezes slowly. Lady Jane Hurstmantle struggles, but to no avail. As she passes into unconsciousness, her killer, quite unperturbed, whispers a message into her ear.

"Thomas Cromwell sends his regards, My Lady Hurstmantle."

*

Outside the gardens of Hurstmantle House, Rafe Sadler stands guard, and holds onto the horses. Master Cromwell usually likes to have someone watch as a scheme unfolds. It usually bonds his young men together. Tonight will be a little different.

Minutes go by, and Rafe is becoming unsettled. Then Drew Jennings appears from the gloom, striding towards him. Behind him, flames are licking out of the great house's windows. Lady Jane is known to like a candle in the night, and that can be a dangerous thing.

"Accident waiting to happen. Such an awful shame," Thomas Cromwell will say to the king, and he with a stiff letter already drawn up to sign. "Such a pity that she never felt your anger, sire."

The king will sigh, and speak of the fickleness of fate, or give a rambling discourse on the cruel vagaries of bad luck. Then he will forget all about his old lover, and recall only that she had betrayed him, and so her end cannot be decried too loudly.

"Is it done?" Rafe asks, as Jennings comes up to him. In the moonlight his face is that of a demon, and he smiles thinly at Cromwell's ginger haired little lawyer. The man is nervous, even holding the horses, and Jennings wonders if the rest are as weak.

"It is," Drew Jennings replies. He might add how much he enjoyed the gruesome double murder, but he does not. He doubts Rafe Sadler would approve of the pleasure to be had from ill using a frightened victim. It is, he thinks, an acquired taste. "They died in they sleep."

"They?"

"She had a lover with her in bed," Drew Jennings explains. "Though Master Cromwell need not think I want paying twice. We must consider the young man to be an unlucky victim, doomed by his own vices. No loss."

"We should leave now," Rafe says, as the flames lick about the house's wooden structure. "See, the servants are awake, and they are looking to quell the flames."

"They seek to spoil our sport," Jennings replies, with a cackling laugh.

"You want to stay and watch?" Rafe asks.

Drew Jennings could explain how much pleasure he gets from watching a fire consuming flesh, or the joy of abusing a terrified victim, but he forebears. Sadler is, he thinks, a weakling.

Instead, he crosses to the nearest horse, and raises his left foot to the stirrup. Rafe Sadler is close behind him, and they are framed between the moonlight, and the leaping flames. He draws his dagger, and drives it up into Drew Jennings' unguarded back. As the man slumps down, Rafe bends, and whispers a message into his ear.

"Best regards, from Tom Cromwell."

*

"God bless the bride and groom!" Thomas Cromwell raises a glass and toasts the happy couple. In the few short weeks he has known Will Draper he has come to be very fond of the man. If he were more honest with himself, he might realise that it is because of the similarity between them.

"Thank you, Master Cromwell," Will replies. "Miriam and I pledge ourselves to your service, and thank you for your great munificence."

"Munificence is it?" Richard Cromwell laughs, and stuffs a piece of wild duck flesh into his ever hungry mouth. "Why, I swear you are the most well read, and learned soldier I have ever come across. I wager you used to be a damned Romish priest... not a fighting man."

Will takes this in good part, but the lack of a real past is a constant thorn in his side. It is one thing to be well educated by a kindly old priest, but quite another to think he might be your father. The son of a priest, and a trained killer is not a happy combination to live with, and he hopes his character is formed more by the former, rather than the latter.

"The king!" someone shouts, and the entire company loyally repeats the toast.

"No... I am from the king!" the young page shouts over the hubbub of happy noise. "I have an urgent message from His Majesty."

"What is it boy?" Cromwell asks, as he dabs at his lips.

"The king has need of you, Master Cromwell," the lad says. "The French ambassador has just arrived, and he wishes to speak with you, urgently, before granting him an audience."

"See how highly thought of I am," Cromwell says to his nephew.

"Shall I come with you, uncle?" Richard asks.

"No, stay for the feast," Cromwell says. "If I cannot handle the king with my wits, then yours will not help me any the more"

Thomas Cromwell stands, and waits for his lad to fetch a fur cloak. It is very cold outside, and he must stay warm, if he is to manage the king's affairs of state.

"A month ago, they thought he would end on the gallows," Mush says to his new brother-in-law. "Now, those same men say he will try to rule the king."

"Give him time," Will Draper replies, with a smile. "Whatever course he runs, we will be with him. Perhaps he will end up making England over in his own image. So, as I say …give him time."

Afterword

Thank you for reading this book. It is, of course, a work of fiction, hung on a skeleton of fact, and should be judged as such.

*

The house at Austin Friars is a real place. It was taken over by Thomas Cromwell, and used by him throughout his life. In the period from 1529 to 1540, the house was used as a government office, as well as a private home.

*

York Place was the elegant town house of Cardinal Wolsey, who lost it to Henry at the time of his fall from grace (c1529). During the next few years, it became known as 'Whitehall', and grew in size, until it contained almost 1,500 rooms. During the decade inquisition, it acted as a centre of power, alongside Westminster, and Hampton Court Palace.

*

Will Draper's sword is of Germanic origin. The description given, is for one often used by soldiers of the Emperor Charles V's guard, and was in wide use throughout Europe between 1520 and 1540. That such a sword might end up on an Irish battlefield is entirely possible. English armies of invasion comprised mercenaries from all nations, with entire companies of Genoese, Flemish, French, German and Welsh incorporated.

*

The discriminatory edict against the Jewish race survived for about four hundred years in England, and robbed the country of access to a vast amount of European, and middle eastern, culture. Many Jewish men of business risked death by trading in London, under the guise of being Spanish or Flemish traders, and their religion was demonised right up until the reign of Charles II.

*

From 1530 onwards, Henry's reign became increasingly bloody. His quest for a son changed the face of Europe for ever.

Anne Stevens

Winter King is the first volume in the Tudor Crimes cycle, and the adventures of Will Draper and Thomas Cromwell continue with:

Midnight Queen
The Stolen Prince
The Condottiero
The King's Angels
The King's Examiner,
The Alchemist Royal
A Twilight of Queens
A Falcon Falls
A King's Ransom
Autumn Prince
The Abyssinian
A Cardinal Sin
Traitor's Gate
 A Mercy of Kings

All exclusively available through Amazon Kindle, and in printed format from 2017.

TightCircle Publications

The Black Jigsaw is a dark slice of the underbelly of pre-war crime, and leads the reader through a maze of corruption, kidnap, brutality, and murder.

This is the debut novel of Tessa Dale, and features the incorruptible DCI Trask, and his quest to find an evil child abductor, before he can strike again. His path to ultimate justice is strewn with wickedly contrived sub-plots, and his methodology is a joy to read about.

DCI Trask is a man of his time, and Tessa Dale has created him with some considerable skill. The setting, 1930s pre-war England, is most evocatively drawn, and each character feels as real as can be.

'A startlingly good debut' .....

'You can taste the evil in every page, and DCI Trask is the square jawed avenger.' .....

'The best pipe smoking detective since Holmes..'

King's Quest is the latest novel by Anne Stevens, and follows the turbulent life and times of Luke Boyd in Georgian England.

As a small boy, he is raised in the wild frontier land between Canada, and the newly emerging United Staes of America. He grows up fighting for his place in the world, against rebel Americans, intent on pushing the British out of Canada, and the murderous Iraquios tribes along the border.

Luke becomes a consummate killer of men, and attracts the attentions of William McCloud, English gentleman, and master spy. The king has need of good men to fight against the ever more powerful Napoleon, men who can go into the lion's den.

Luke joins McCloud's secret band, and they set out on an adventure that might change the world. Their chaotic journey from Montréal to Kew sees them locking horns with French agents, being bribed by the Prince of Wales   - known to all as 'Fat Prinny', calling on William Pitt, and finding their way into the royal palace at Kew.

Mad King George, swinging between a tenuous grip on sanity, and a consuming madness he must fight, holds the key to a dark secret…

Anne Stevens at her best……Bel Ami

Printed in Great Britain
by Amazon

81470335R00192